THE

Babylonian Quartet

THE FURNACE THE RESTORATION THE DEN

J. Clarke McIntosh

WESTBOW
PRESS®
A DIVISION OF THOMAS NELSON
& ZONDERVAN

WestBow Press books may be ordered through booksellers or by contacting:

WestBow Press
A Division of Thomas Nelson & Zondervan
1663 Liberty Drive
Bloomington, IN 47403
www.westbowpress.com
844-714-3454

ISBN: 978-1-6642-6168-6 (sc)
ISBN: 978-1-6642-6169-3 (hc)
ISBN: 978-1-6642-6167-9 (e)

Library of Congress Control Number: 2022905351

Print information available on the last page.

WestBow Press rev. date: 4/22/2022

I dedicate this book to my siblings:

W. Scott McIntosh (my twin)
R. Lawton McIntosh
Jane McIntosh McRoy

For more information about my work, I encourage you to go to HRNT. org and scroll down to missionary staff

It is worthwhile to pause upon the point, for nothing has been so wholly missed in our modern religious ideals as the ideal of tenacity …The ideal was out of date almost from the first day; that is why it is eternal, for whatever is dated is doomed.

—GK Chesterton. *The New Jerusalem*

PREFACE

J. R. R. Tolkien spoke often of true myth. They are true stories that are mythical in scope beyond the normal ken of our lives. One of the books in the Bible with a superabundance of true myth is Daniel. In our pseudo-sophistication, modern skeptics scornfully laugh at the stories from Daniel, dismissing them by grouping them with fairy tales and fables. Even those of faith are often embarrassed by stories of supernatural revelation and interpretation of other people's dreams, such as surviving super-heated furnaces and sleeping with lions. We relegate those stories to children's Sunday school classes; too often we feel no desire to hear them again because they are so familiar, and because they are so mythical, miraculous, inexplicable.

For many years, I limited my personal devotional time to the study of New Testament books. I felt that God only spoke to his people through that more complete revelation, even though when Paul touted the value of the scriptures, he was referring to the Torah or Old Testament. Daniel was the first Old Testament book that I studied in depth. I was amazed at how God spoke to me through those pages. Of course, the stories were familiar. What child in America does not know about Daniel in the lions' den and the three Hebrew boys surviving Nebuchadnezzar's furnace? However, I was surprised at how much this overly familiar book addressed my needs and blessed me at a critical juncture in my life.

Jesus warned us that unless we come to him as children, we cannot come at all. If we think that we are too mature for the truths that God reveals in this book or too sophisticated to revisit inexplicable miracles, we need to be reintroduced to Daniel. We need to empathize with the adolescent boys snatched from their homes and planted in a foreign culture. We need to emulate the four young men who became brothers and supported one another as they gave themselves to excellence and used to give in to the severe pressure to compromise, even though they found themselves exiled in a hostile, pagan land. We need to stand with them as we read about their refusal to deny their faith in the face of imminent danger. We need to rejoice like Nebuchadnezzar did when he found the one true God, even if it takes devastating humiliation to bring us to that point. I hope that Azariah (Abed-Nego) speaks to you through this book, for we still need his instruction and experience in our lives. I do, at any rate.

GLOSSARY OF TERMS

Adonai. The spoken form of holy name of God, YHWH, which is too holy to be spoken.

Bar. Aramaic for son of, like Simon Bar Jonah, when used in a name.

Canaan. The Promised Land, an inheritance promised to Abraham and conquered by Joshua.

Davidic line. Those in the lineage for the throne of King David of Israel.

Levite. Temple worker from the tribe of Levi and not a priest or descendant of Aaron.

Mammon. Riches and power in this world.

Priest. Jewish religious leader from the tribe of Levi who descended from Aaron.

Sheol. Death, the grave, and sometimes interpreted as hell.

Stadia. The plural of stadium, one-eighth of a mile, 220 yards (200 meters), and a furlough.

Synagogue. Jewish place of worship if there are more than ten families in a town.

Talent. A unit of weight. A Talent of gold was fifteen years' wages

The Great Sea. The Mediterranean (Middle of the Earth) Sea.

Time. A twelve-hour day: the first hour (6:00 am.), the sixth hour (noon), and the twelfth hour (6:00 pm.).

Torah. Can mean either the first five books of the Old Testament or the entire Old Testament. It is sometimes called the Law and the Prophets.

Book One
THE FURNACE

P ROLOGUE. KING JOSIAH WAS THE ONE BRIGHT LIGHT IN AN otherwise dismal constellation of Judah's kings who followed in the wake of the great King Hezekiah. Judah was led into apostasy by King Manasseh and King Amon. The faithful and encouraging reign of King Josiah was followed by the disastrous reign of King Jehoiakim. Numerous great prophets (Isaiah, Jeremiah, Ezekiel, Habakkuk) had threatened the coming of the wrath of God, but it finally fell upon Judah in the form of the Chaldean army when King Nebuchadnezzar captured Jerusalem. Though he was incensed by the defiance of King Jehoiakim, the Chaldean monarch sought to build up his realm rather than destroy the vanquished. Instead of killing the brightest and best from the lands that he conquered, Nebuchadnezzar took them to Babylon. His plan was to discern the most fitting and accomplished from among the exiles in order to incorporate them into the Chaldean culture. Perhaps if they were exceptional, they would go into the court of Nebuchadnezzar. This is the story of four such young men.

1

CHAPTER ONE

A Leader Emerges

ON THE MORNING OF OUR TWELFTH DAY OF TRAVEL, WE crested a hill and got our first glimpse of the city that would become our new home. I stood in awe, gazing at the tremendous expanse before us. Babylon was far bigger than I had ever conceived or imagined. We were looking at a real city for the first time. All of us were struck dumb and immobile.

Though my father had been appointed to Jerusalem and spent a significant amount of his time in the Jewish capital, I had spent the majority of my life in Hebron. I was far more familiar with rural activities, such as shepherding and harvesting wheat and barley than I was with the pursuits of the city. My rustic roots were exposed when I had ventured into Jerusalem for the first time; I had been amazed at the vastness of the city and the multitude of people who had been crowded into such a small area. I had wondered why people willingly chose to live in such a confined environment.

However, we were now poised to enter Babylon, which was the capital of the Chaldean empire and perhaps the greatest city in the world. With my first glance, I realized that Jerusalem could easily be annexed to Babylon and no one would notice the addition. As we approached the gaping gates of the great city, it felt like we were about to be consumed by the Chaldean capital.

There were four of us traveling together—a recently formed quartet. Our trek to Babylon had started as a jumble of men and soldiers, but on the third day, I had found myself traveling in the company of three youths. My companions and I were herded together by the eldest youth in the quartet, a lad named Daniel, who was about two years older than me. Daniel took steps to bring us together because he had had a vision from God of what the future held for him and his companions. His selecting and directing us together was the first experience that I had of his leadership, but we were destined to learn to trust this unusual youth, who possessed the wisdom and drive of a man far beyond his years. Daniel had introduced me to Hananiah and Mishael. All of us were distantly related through the Davidic line, though Mishael and Hananiah were much closer to the kingly throne of David than Daniel or me.

My name is Azariah. That journey occurred at a difficult period of my life. My father, Asher, had recently died while defending Jerusalem from Nebuchadnezzar and the Chaldeans, the most powerful army in the world. The Chaldeans had conquered our country three years earlier, but our foolish king, Jehoiakim, had provoked our conquerors by withholding our tribute and bringing their ire upon us. My father led Judah's troops to intercept the Chaldean forces so that our leaders would have more time to negotiate a conditional surrender to Nebuchadnezzar. Abba and his men fought valiantly, but died in the desperate struggle because of foul-ups by the king. King Jehoiakim was taken captive and was led in chains to Babylon, but our quartet was selected because of our perceived intelligence and leadership potential. When we reached the Chaldean capital, we were to be trained in the Chaldean history, language, and customs. After the schooling, we would be tested to see if we were good enough to become counselors in the court of Nebuchadnezzar.

As we continued on our journey, Daniel became the leader of our group as a matter of course. Not only was he the eldest (Hananiah and Mishael were about my age), but he also exuded the confidence that was required of a good leader. He had the charisma to attract others. He combined this with true interest and concern for people. When he spoke to a person about any matter of importance, the individual knew that Daniel was not feigning interest. Instead, you felt that nothing mattered to our leader at that time except hearing and understanding your response. In addition, we would find out that Daniel's faith was the bedrock of his life. During our trek, the three of us grew to admire and trust our new leader. This admiration would grow steadily.

Up to the day that we entered Babylon, the temple of Solomon was the greatest structure that I had ever beheld, but Nebuchadnezzar's palace was at least twice as high and four times as large. Though the palace was the largest structure in Babylon, there were probably fifty buildings as large as our temple, the greatest structure in all of Jerusalem and Judea. However, it was not only the vastness of the city and the size of the buildings that astounded me. Babylon overwhelmed our senses in every possible manner.

As we drew nearer, we felt the noise of the city as much as we heard it. As we entered the city gates, the beat and roar reached its crescendo. Shortly after entering those gates, we turned sharply to the left. We were confronted by the enormous palace itself. Hananiah pointed to the right and declared, "Look...there. It's the famous hanging gardens." He never explained how he knew about those wonders, but as I followed his gaze, I saw plots of land suspended in the air with flowers, fruits, vegetables exploding from their bases. About that time, the smells of the city assaulted me with the vile, pungent odors of sweat, rotting produce, and dung, which liberally littered the streets. The roar of Babylon distilled into the sounds of the city: shouting, bleating, neighing, and cursing. Our minds were in a whirl.

We had made the journey from Jerusalem to Babylon on foot, but when we arrived in the Chaldean capital, we were overwhelmed by the vast number of vehicles. Pedestrians were still in the majority, of course; the streets were jammed with people seeking to buy or hawk wares, carrying bundles, and herding livestock. But what seemed unfathomable to me were the vehicles. Never had I seen so many carriages and horses in my life. Until that time, I'd been impressed with the number of vehicles in Jerusalem. My father owned a nice carriage in which we often rode in Jerusalem. On our journeys, we typically met other vehicles when we were out, but at other times, we had the only carriage on the road for a substantial part of our journey. At those times, it was enough of an

event to meet another carriage, even in the middle of Jerusalem, that
we often stopped and carried on a conversation for several minutes. No
one in Babylon stopped to talk. In fact, no one seemed to talk, although
shouting was abundant. Everyone seemed to be in a constant hurry. If
a carriage stopped unnecessarily, the driver was pelted with curses and
sometimes with rotten produce until he moved on.

Ashpenaz, the captain of the guard who was appointed by
Nebuchadnezzar to select and transport choice youths from Judea, was
amused as we gawked at our surroundings while he guided us to our
new homes. During the journey, my mind had often wandered as I
contemplated what life among the Chaldeans would be like. I had no
experience that was solid enough to either launch me into daydreams
of ecstasy or precipitate great consternation. In many ways, my mind
was like an empty slate as we ventured forth. Now the slate was being
inscribed upon.

We were led to a large courtyard with multiple dwellings crammed
side by side. Each building was large and appeared to be richly endowed.
Though the four of us came from affluent families by Jerusalem's
standards, none of us had ever seen such luxurious apartments, but
their richness was not the kind that I would have chosen. Drapes and
pillows were scattered everywhere. The beds were soft, and there were
no chairs. The tables were low to the ground; we were supposed to eat
while sitting on the cushions. All of it felt strange but welcoming. It was
comforting to realize that we had completed our journey and that we
were now "home." We were young; we could adjust to new ways.

Shortly after our arrival, Daniel gathered the quartet together.
"Though I can't speak for the three of you, I'm overwhelmed and
intimidated by everything around us. Babylon is much larger than I
ever imagined. After speaking with the guards in my broken Chaldean,
it's clear that the king and his advisors expect us to become Chaldeans
and adopt their ways. We're to learn their language and literature, and
I foresee no problems in committing ourselves to seek to excel in those
areas." He paused and took our measure.

"Though I have no desire to begin my new life here in conflict with
the leaders, there are some lines I must draw from the start, and I want
you to understand me. If they attempt to make us worship the Chaldean

gods—and there are reasons for me to think that they might—I'll have to take a firm stance. It's not fair for me to make a decision for each of you, but I hope you'll feel the same way. Though we should seek to befriend those over us and cooperate in every possible way that we can, I feel compelled to worship the God of Abraham, Isaac, Jacob, and him alone. I won't worship any other god, and I will not refrain from worshiping Adonai, no matter what the consequences are. I can't and won't worship the gods of the Chaldeans, for in the depth of my soul, I am convinced that Adonai, the God of Israel, is the only legitimate deity. Though I hope the three of you will join me, I'll stand alone if necessary. We're in a foreign land; in many areas I can adjust the way I live, but I must remain faithful to Adonai, the God of Abraham, Isaac, and Jacob. That is an issue for which I'm willing to die."

The depth of conviction and commitment behind Daniel's statement impressed me greatly. Though I, too, worshiped the God of Israel alone and was unwilling to worship foreign gods, I would have been reticent to take such a vocal and unbending stance before companions that I had just met, especially just as we were arriving in this new land. Daniel's courage and commitment goaded me to join him in his commitment.

As soon as Daniel concluded, I replied, "You're right, Daniel. Though I'm willing to be flexible in some areas, I cannot adopt the Chaldean religion. If I'm put to the test, I'll refuse to worship the pagan gods and continue to worship Adonai. If for no other reason, I won't compromise my beliefs because I know I'd disappoint my Abba too greatly. Though he's dead, I feel his presence with me, goading me on to follow his example. If they try to force us to worship their gods or deny our faith in Adonai, I'll stand with you, even if it means our death. Abba went to battle, knowing it would probably be his death. I cannot disappoint him by being less resolute."

Hananiah and Mishael were a bit more hesitant initially. Their reluctance was not surprising. They were influenced by the same family pressures that caused King Jehoiakim to forsake our faith. Eventually, however, they both voiced their commitment. Each declared his willingness to defy our masters if pushed to worship Chaldean gods, even if it meant his death. In the end, I believe the primary force that swayed them was Daniel's commitment and charisma. We were all attracted to him like moths to light. Whatever their initial motivation, once Hananiah and Mishael committed themselves, their stance was as firm as bedrock, as they proved over the years.

Shortly after our arrival, we were given Chaldean names, but I never have been able to discern their motivation for this step. Was our renaming to welcome us and give us a feeling of kinship as though we were Chaldeans or to dishearten us by taking away our Hebrew identities? In truth, they were probably motivated by a mixture of the two. Daniel was given the name Belteshazzar. Hananiah was dubbed Shadrach. Mishael was called Meshach. They gave me the name Abed-nego. Although I had initially despised the adulteration of my name, my Chaldean name was my identity for so long in my official capacity that I now rather liked the sound. Though I preferred Azariah, the name my parents gave me, I answered readily to both names.

We had been settled in Babylon for less than a fortnight when our first challenge arose. The issue was subtle and unexpected. Indeed, I probably would have let this challenge slip by without taking notice, but the gift from Nebuchadnezzar sounded bells of alarm in Daniel. As Jews, we had strict culinary laws and customs. The challenge we faced centered on the food we would consume. As I have contemplated what had occurred, I felt almost certain that King Nebuchadnezzar had no intention of causing us distress. His desire was to enhance our chances to succeed and compete with the other youths—even the Chaldeans. Whatever his motivation, the king stirred up consternation in our household when he ordered food from his cooks to be given to all the youths that had been brought into Babylon. The diet of the king violated our culinary restrictions in virtually every conceivable way. Moreover, the wine from the king's table was far more potent than the diluted wine that we had grown up drinking.

When we learned about the king's gift, Daniel convened another council. "Though I hate to take a controversial stance so quickly after our arrival, I cannot in good conscience eat the food that Nebuchadnezzar has ordered his cook to provide for us. Though being faithful in observing our diet may seem like a small thing, I think that's how faithfulness or unfaithfulness starts. As we learn to be faithful in small things, we'll be ready when more difficult challenges arise."

Hananiah replied, "Aren't we getting a bit carried away? Though I agree with your desire to be faithful and remain true to our heritage, I have no desire to become a zealot. If you'd ever eaten with King Jehoiakim, you would have found the same cuisine the king has ordered. What Nebuchadnezzar is sending to us is really just the diet of kings. The food has nothing to do with our Jewish heritage or laws."

I countered, "Well I, for one, would hardly look to King Jehoiakim as an example for us to emulate in any area, particularly adhering to the laws of Adonai or the customs of our people. He blatantly disregarded all of God's laws and worshiped Phoenician idols, so it's hardly surprising that he cared nothing for the restrictions on diet. On the other hand, I agree with Hananiah's underlying sentiment. Are we really going to risk insulting the king by refusing his food? Is there no way to find a compromise to avoid making ourselves odious over something that's relatively insignificant?"

Daniel looked at Mishael and asked, "Do you want to comment or contribute an opinion?" After Mishael shook his head, Daniel continued, "Azariah's point is intelligent. We should respect it. If the three of you will permit me to be your representative, I'll speak to Hathach, the one appointed to watch over us and bring us our food. Let me make an appeal to him to try and work out something agreeable to both sides."

Because Daniel thought my question showed insight and sensitivity, even with its implied doubt, he took me with him. In the interview that followed, Daniel impressed me with the respect and sincerity he implemented during his negotiations. "Commander Hathach, we understand that King Nebuchadnezzar is being generous by sending us food from his table. Though we have no desire to be obstinate, the food he wants to give us is far richer than what we're accustomed to. Many of the foods go against the laws and customs of our people. We'd prefer to have more vegetables and water."

Despite Daniel's gentle words, Hathach responded irately, "Why do you want to make trouble for me? I wish that my only dilemma was figuring out how to deal with such overt generosity from the king. Nebuchadnezzar has commanded this food to be given to you out of the kindness and generosity of his heart, and I plan to bring it to you. If you refuse to eat it, that's your issue. However, if I give you only vegetables and water, you'll grow weak and haggard looking, and that will cause the king's anger to be poured out upon me. Indeed, I could lose my head."

Daniel responded, "We understand your concerns. Truly, we don't seek to make trouble for you. Let's set up a trial as a kind of compromise. Bring us the food we request for ten days. If we eat the food of our culture and stay strong, all will be well. We can remain faithful to our God and Jewish culture without getting you in trouble. If we've grown weak and our appearance worsens, we'll stop the trial and eat the king's food without complaint." Though he remained unconvinced, Hathach agreed to the trial.

After the ten days were completed, Hathach fulfilled the spirit of the trial by comparing us to our colleagues, although the results had been obvious for days. Our color was better; we were far more vigorous and robust. Many of those who ate the king's food and drank his wine looked bloated, pale, and lethargic. There was really no contest as to which group looked better. In addition to avoiding the foods that so violated our culture, one of the best outcomes of that interaction was that Hathach became loyal to us. Because of the courtesy Daniel had shown him, he sought to help us in any legitimate way that he could.

The next eighteen months in our lives involved strenuous application to the tasks at hand. Nebuchadnezzar's plan was for us to study the Chaldean culture and language for three years. We applied ourselves with proper diligence, and Adonai blessed us in multiple ways. Daniel, our unofficial leader, declared that our primary emphasis should be pleasing God, so we structured our days to reflect our priorities. Every evening, we prayed and spent time reminding ourselves of our Jewish heritage and the God of Israel's faithfulness while dealing with his people through the years. Daniel led many of the sessions, but he called on each of us to take part.

In order to make a good impression before my colleagues—particularly Daniel—I prepared diligently when it was my turn to lead. I think each of us felt that way. The preparation forced us to recall and contemplate the lessons that we had learned as youths in Jerusalem and apply that knowledge to our current situation. After about an hour or so, we reviewed our lessons from the day. Each of us took turns rehashing the lessons and coming up with helpful and probing questions, which led to in-depth discussions. After about three months, we started using the Chaldean tongue when we reviewed our lessons so that our studies served a dual purpose. By that method, our language skills improved as rapidly as our knowledge of Chaldean literature and wisdom.

Clearly, God blessed our efforts. Not only did we master the literature and wisdom of the Chaldeans; we also became fluent in the language much faster than the other exiles. Within a year, the four of us stood out from the rest of those who were enrolled in the lessons—both exiles and Chaldean students. Unexpectedly, God also gave us the ability to understand visions and dreams. Those gifts were present in each of us, but they were most pronounced in Daniel. He had some experience in interpreting dreams before we were transported to Babylon, but as we applied ourselves to our studies and sought to please the Lord, those gifts became more obvious in our leader. What none of us realized at the time was that Daniel's special giftedness in that area would play an immense role in our survival and function within the realm of the Babylonians.

CHAPTER TWO

The Great Dream

Back in Jerusalem, when Ashpenaz started selecting youths, none of the four of us aspired to be chosen. Though it was impossible for my ego not to be stroked by the words that Ashpenaz employed while describing those he sought—youths with intelligence, strength, stamina, handsome appearance, and strong character—my overarching desire at the time was to elude selection by the Chaldeans. We had talked enough among us that I realized that each of my companions had similar feelings. Daniel had been an inevitable choice because he was smarter, stronger, handsomer, more athletic than all other youths of Jerusalem. Hananiah and Mishael thought like I did that there was some chance they could avoid selection. In the end, all four of us were chosen. Because we understood the power and wisdom of Adonai, we accepted that we were there by his design, so we diligently applied ourselves, both in our contemplation and remembrance of Adonai and the comprehension of our Chaldean studies.

By the middle of the three years that had been appointed for our education, our quartet had distinguished ourselves sufficiently from the rest of our group that we received special recognition. In an unprecedented maneuver, we were ingrafted into Nebuchadnezzar's court even before completing our training. By the end of the second year of our exile, we were promoted to the position of junior members of

Nebuchadnezzar's council. Even during the final year of our education, we were numbered among the wise men of the Chaldeans. We were cognizant of the honor that was afforded to us, but we did not realize the danger that the promotion entailed.

Toward the end of our second year in Babylon, King Nebuchadnezzar had an important dream. He was concerned, and all of Babylon was disturbed with him, for he transferred his distress to his counselors. I have had dreams that seemed vivid and important, yet upon waking, they had seemed just beyond the reach of my conscious recall. Despite my best efforts to recall the nocturnal vision, I could not bring to mind the details of the dream, so I could empathize with the plight of the monarch. Though I never had confirmation of my conjecture, I am convinced that is what happened to the Babylonian ruler.

Nebuchadnezzar assembled his most experienced sages, told them his dilemma, and enlisted their aid. From his exalted height on the throne, the king declared, "Most distinguished sages and wise men, I'm presenting you with a conundrum. I am placing upon you a command that will either prove to be a great opportunity to distinguish the greatest and most worthy among you or that will be the undoing of all my counselors." He paused, scanning his counselors as he allowed his message to be driven home. "Two nights ago, I was awakened by a dream of such magnitude and majesty that I'm certain it was a message sent to me from the gods. Since you are my sages and the wisest of my subjects, I am commanding you to tell me the dream and its interpretation." Nebuchadnezzar sat stock-still on his throne as he slowly scanned his audience. His face was like that of a statue as he surveyed the countenances of his most experienced sages.

Teresh, one of the most revered of the wise men, stepped before the king and said, "Thank you for this opportunity, most exalted and beneficent king. Tell us the dream, and we'll render the interpretation." He stood expectantly, looking at the king.

Suddenly the statue exploded into life. The irate king exclaimed, "Don't play games with me or treat me like a fool, Teresh. My command is as firm as I have given it. Either you tell me the dream and then the interpretation or face the consequences. I have selected each of you because of the perceived intelligence and insight that has been given to you by the gods. If I have truly wise and enlightened counselors, you'll be able to recite the dream and its interpretation to me. The man who succeeds will be exalted above all the men in my realm, second only to me. He will receive houses, lands, promotion, and untold wealth. His position will become the envy of all his peers. However, if all my sages disappoint me in this critical juncture, I'll execute every one of the supposedly wise men of my court and try to find some new, truly insightful counselors, for you'll have failed me when I needed you most."

The countenances of Teresh and all his comrades fell as they heard the declaration of the king. "Oh wise and most exalted king, your commands are our first priorities and the greatest desires of our souls. We live to obey and fulfill all the commands and requests that come from your throne, but today, you make a demand that no mortal man can fulfill. From the beginning of time, no king has placed such an expectation on his subjects, for it is beyond the capabilities of man. How can one man know the dreams of another? Only the gods can give you a satisfactory answer to your dilemma. The gods sent the dream that disturbed your sleep. Only they can show the dream and the interpretation to another being." All the sages who were present nodded in agreement with Teresh and then bowed before the king.

"Has Teresh spoken for all of you? Is there no one among you who can give me satisfaction in this inquiry?" After waiting some time for a positive response to his inquiry, Nebuchadnezzar muttered to himself, "Why should I let such fools darken my courts and consume my food?" Then he raised his head and stared down at each of his counselors as he announced with authority, "If you cannot help me when I have a true dilemma, it would be better for me to slay the lot of you and train up some truly wise counselors who can serve the realm when serious questions arise. Go home and pray to your gods to give you the insight I demand, for you are sorely trying my patience. When my patience is exhausted, I'll bring each of you before my throne. If you cannot solve my dilemma, I can at least obtain some satisfaction by watching each of you die. My decree is final. Leave my presence and pray with all your strength to your gods. If you cannot give me a satisfactory answer soon—very soon—prepare your souls for death." Then the king dismissed them from his presence.

Nebuchadnezzar sent Arioch, the captain of his bodyguards, to inform all of the wise men and sages of the sentence that the king had imposed upon them. When Arioch came to us, he declared, "My Hebrew friends, I have sorrowful news to impart. Each of you must put your souls in order, for your days are numbered. The king has placed an impossible request upon all his wise men. Unfortunately, the sentence of death is upon you as well the other sages and Chaldeans. The hard work that resulted in your early promotion to be numbered among the wise men of Babylon will prove to be your undoing. The king has declared that all his sages are sentenced to death because none of you can help him in his great dilemma."

Instead of panicking, Daniel responded to the captain. "What is this grave dilemma? What can none of his wise men address? What conundrum will result in our deaths?"

Turning a melancholy countenance upon our leader, Arioch replied, "The king had a dream three days ago. He's declared that anyone who can tell him the dream and its interpretation shall be honored and exalted to the highest position in his entire realm, inferior to him only. However, if none of his sages and wise men can tell him the dream and its interpretation, they're a disappointment to him. He'll slay all his counselors and start afresh." With that, Arioch told us all that had occurred between the king and his counselors. "Harsh as it is, the king has made a firm declaration. He won't rescind it. His demands have been placed upon all his counselors; there will be no exceptions. However, who can satisfy such a challenge? Only the gods possess such wisdom. Therefore, you must use these next few days to prepare your souls to meet death."

Returning the gaze of the messenger, Daniel declared, "Arioch, we're servants of Adonai, the all-powerful, omniscient God. We don't share your pessimism or the despondency of our colleagues. Though the king has made a firm declaration, we don't consider the command of the king to be outside the realm of possibility. The giving and interpretation of dreams belongs to Adonai, the One True God of Israel. Please petition the king to give us time so that we can tell the king the dream and its interpretation. Adonai will show us the truth to spare our lives. He'll demonstrate to you and all those in Nebuchadnezzar's court that he is the One True God." Daniel spoke confidently, surprising his messenger.

After a momentary pause, Arioch replied to Daniel, "Be careful, my young friend. Nebuchadnezzar isn't a man with whom to trifle. If you're merely stalling, trying to gain a few more days or hoping the king will change his mind, you'd do better to accept the sentence of death, for the king won't relent. He can devise tortures that will make you wish your grandfather had never been born."

"We're not stalling. Each of us knows too well that King Nebuchadnezzar must be treated with respect, but we also know that all wisdom and knowledge belong to the God of Israel. In the past, Adonai has revealed the interpretation of dreams to me. He's able to tell us both the dream and its interpretation. Get the king to give us time to fast and pray before the Lord. We're confident that Adonai will reveal the secret to us," replied Daniel. "Get the king to delay the executions until we've had a chance to call upon our God."

Arioch left our abode and hurried to the king. Having stewed in his vexation at the unresponsiveness of his wise men, Nebuchadnezzar was irate. Though he had planned to start the executions the following day, the message from Daniel stayed his hand.

As one can readily imagine, we prayed and fasted in earnest, knowing that unless the Lord was merciful to us, we faced a horrible death. Adonai proved gracious and faithful to us. In the evening of the second day, Adonai revealed the dream and interpretation to Daniel. When he was certain that the Lord had answered our prayers, Daniel led us in praise to the God of Israel. "Let the name of Adonai be praised forever, for all wisdom and power belong to him. He is truly the only omniscient and omnipotent one. He sets up kingdoms and brings them to naught. He brings down those who exalt themselves and lifts up the humble. Out of the abundance of his grace, he has answered our prayers; by his mighty hand, he has spared our lives. To him alone belongs the power to reveal profound mysteries and make things that are hidden known. Though all is darkness to man, God sees all. He reveals hidden mysteries to his subjects when it pleases him to do so."

Early the following morning, I went to fetch Arioch to tell him the good news. When I arrived, there were about one hundred wise men sitting in the outer courts of the palace, looking dejected, forlorn, dismayed. As I entered, I overheard a confidential conversation between two of the Chaldeans. "These are our last days, but I'm in no mood to partake of a festive last meal. I have no intention of going out in style. The executions might as well have already occurred, for there's no joy in our hearts. Sitting under the sentence of death is worse than lying in Sheol. Who would have expected the final days of our lives to arrive so quickly? Who would've thought that when I worked so hard to become a counselor in the court of Nebuchadnezzar, I was bringing a death sentence upon my head?"

His companion replied, "What makes you so despondent? Those Hebrew exiles told Arioch that they would have an answer to give to the king. They claim their god will reveal the dream to them so that none of us will have to die."

"Phssh...I think those Hebrew lads may have outsmarted themselves. Can you imagine what Nebuchadnezzar will do to them when their inevitable failure becomes known? Yes, they've come up with a tactic to delay the inevitable, but the eventual outcome will be the same for us and far worse for them than they can possibly imagine. Or are you in such denial that you hold out hope for a genuine answer to the dilemma. I, for one, do not. Even though the king granted this extension, nothing about his previous conduct gives me hope that he will actually give us a final reprieve. His anger at the Hebrew boys may be greater when they disappoint him. They'll die first, and their deaths will be the most heinous. Though his wrath will pour most vehemently upon them, it won't be completely spent. His anger has been stoked to a degree that it will persist even after torturing them to death. Our end will also come without significant delay."

"So, you hold out no hope that the Hebrew's god may reveal the dream?"

The first speaker turned on the second with a look of pity and disdain. "None. I choose not to live in denial. I'll face death as a proud Chaldean rather than pinning my hopes on fairy tales regarding all-knowing gods from other lands."

After listening to this discouraging discourse, I ventured into the court and found Arioch. When I gave him the news, Arioch informed the king of Daniel's declaration so that no executions would take place. Our intervention proved timely; Arioch informed me that the king's patience had been exhausted. The king was contemplating starting the executions that morning, but his hand was stayed by our announcement.

Upon reaching our abode, Arioch asked, "Are you certain that your God has revealed the dream and interpretation? Again, I repeat that if you raise the hopes of the king and then fail, it would've been far better for you to accepted the death that he originally threatened."

Daniel looked at Arioch with utter confidence and declared, "Adonai, the Hebrew God, the God of Abraham, Isaac, and Jacob has revealed the truth to me. If my confidence was founded upon my own wisdom or insight, I would be afraid, but my confidence is in the Lord. I'll tell the king his dream and its interpretation, which God has revealed to me. Adonai has saved our lives and the lives of all the wise men of Babylon. The God of Abraham, Isaac, and Jacob will be honored before you and the king today." Though Arioch looked at our leader in wonder, his countenance reflected his fear and misgivings.

As the four of us traveled back with Arioch, there was irony in our carriage, which was apparent to anyone observing our small band of walkers. Daniel was the one who made his positive declaration that he knew the king's dream and that he could interpret it. He was to stand and deliver it before the most powerful monarch in the world. More than anyone else, he would face the king's wrath if he failed. If his interpretation proved false, he would suffer and wish that he had never been born, but he showed no fear. His posture was upright, and his stride was bold. On his countenance rested a quiet confidence and an assurance that all would be well. Hananiah, Mishael, and I were also confident, although perhaps our assurance was somewhat less apparent than Daniel's. However, Arioch's shoulders drooped, and his head was bowed. He had the appearance of one marching to his death.

When we arrived, we were ushered into that same hall of condemnation—at least, it had seemed that way a few moments earlier—while Arioch informed the king of our arrival. Every eye was fixed on our quartet, but most particularly on Daniel. Word had spread that he was the one who would tell Nebuchadnezzar the dream. A deathly quiet descended upon the room as Arioch beckoned us to proceed into the presence of the Chaldean king. Daniel and Arioch led the procession. We accompanied our companion and leader as he stood before the august king.

Arioch stepped forward, prostrated himself before his monarch, and declared, "Oh, Nebuchadnezzar, most exalted monarch and ruler over all the earth, I've brought to you the Hebrew youths who profess their readiness to tell you both your dream and its interpretation." At that, Arioch crawled back behind the four of us, remaining in the obeisant position without turning his back on the king.

King Nebuchadnezzar sat stoically upon his throne. His visage looked as if it were chiseled from granite. He gazed fiercely at Daniel and then spoke. "Do you have special insight? Are you able to disclose both the dream and its interpretation?"

Though he spoke respectfully, Daniel faced the king boldly, and with no trace of fear in his voice or manner. "Your Highness, no man can know the dreams of another, no matter how wise or insightful he is. If you gave your Chaldean counselors years to discover the truth, they would not have succeeded, nor could I discern your dream on my own. Such wisdom does not reside in the mind of man. However, there is a true God in heaven, the God of the Hebrews. Adonai has made known to me the mysteries that he revealed to you on your bed so that you may have insight as to what the future holds."

"While your sleep was coming to an end, you envisioned a great statue. The statue was exceedingly high and beautiful to behold—indeed, the vision was spectacular, breathtaking to gaze upon. The head of the statue was made of fine gold. The chest and arms were constructed of silver. The abdomen and thighs consisted of bronze. The legs were made of iron, but the feet were a mixture of iron and clay."

As Daniel spoke, I observed the countenance of the king. Nebuchadnezzar had clearly been skeptical initially. His visage was furious when Daniel declared that no man could know the mysteries that the king had demanded to know. However, as Daniel described the statue, the countenance of the king was transformed from rage to amazement. Apparently, Nebuchadnezzar was recognizing and remembering the dream that had eluded him the previous week. His hauteur evaporated as our leader spoke.

Daniel continued, "As you continued to gaze upon the statue, a stone was cut out, yet there were no hands to do the cutting. Then that stone fell upon the statue, crushing it utterly. The portions that were made with iron and clay, the iron, bronze, silver, and gold sections were pulverized and made as chaff before the wind. Simultaneously, the stone grew into a great mountain that dwarfed everything around it. By the end of the dream, the mountain dominated the entire scene." As Daniel paused, the face of the great king showed how accurately Daniel had described his dream. Wonder had replaced his anger and skepticism.

"That was the dream, and this is the interpretation," Daniel declared. "The head of gold is you, Nebuchadnezzar, the greatest king of all the earth, because it has pleased Adonai to make you ruler of all things— all nations, all men, all beasts, even the birds of the air. All things look to you because Adonai, the One True God of Israel, has decreed that it would be so. The Lord has raised you to be his instrument of retribution because of Judah's disobedience and treachery. Your power, rule, and exalted position came to you by the grace of Adonai, but your descendants after you will not be able to keep the kingdom. After your death, the Chaldean realm will fail, but other realms and kings will arise and come to prominence. Though their realms will be extensive, though they will capture much of the territory that you now hold, they will not be equal to the kingdom that you reign over. Those of the silver will give way to those of the bronze. In turn, they will give way to the fourth kingdom, which is the one of iron. As iron is strong and hard, the fourth kingdom will destroy those that preceded it. Then as the rule of that kingdom progresses, its authority will be weakened. Its realm will become less stable, as represented by the feet that are constructed of both iron and clay. Just as iron and clay cannot strongly adhere to one another, the kingdom will inevitably become brittle and eventually be destroyed."

Daniel continued, "The stone cut without hands is the kingdom of Adonai, the One True God. His rule will extend over all realms. Though it will begin small, his kingdom will grow and ascend in power, displacing all that were before it. The kingdom of God will be an eternal kingdom, which will never be displaced. All the kingdoms represented by the statue will fail, but the mountain of the Lord shall prevail. God's kingdom will overwhelm the other kingdoms and endure forever. This, Your Highness, is your dream revealed and interpreted. It is true and trustworthy, for the revelation comes from the one true and living God." When Daniel ceased his narrative, utter silence descended on the room. Again, I looked at the face of Nebuchadnezzar. His countenance was suffused with wonder and awe to an even greater degree than before.

To our amazement and the complete dismay of Arioch, Nebuchadnezzar stepped down from his throne, got down on his knees, and bowed down before Daniel. The great king declared, "Praise be to Daniel, and praise be to Daniel's God. Surely, the God of the Hebrews is the One True God, for he has revealed mysteries that no man could ever discern through his own wisdom and effort. Adonai is true, and you are his true servant, for he has revealed his mystery to me through you." Then the king arose, embraced Daniel, and kissed him on each cheek. He sent Arioch out with the welcome news that the sentence of death had been commuted. Daniel had revealed the mystery—both the dream and its interpretation—thus sparing the lives of all the king's counselors.

CHAPTER THREE

Promotion and Trial

THOUGH KING NEBUCHADNEZZAR COULD JUSTLY HAVE been called a tyrannical ruler, when he made a vow, the promise was solid. The following day before a great assembly and with the royal family, nobles of Babylon, sages, and counselors, he reviewed the proceedings of the previous week. If I were to presume to read the thoughts of men, it appeared that those in attendance were familiar with the story of the king's dream and the demand that he had placed upon his sages long before that gathering, but he repeated the details of the saga for all. The king faithfully told of his dream and threats to the sages. Then he told of Daniel's assurance to Arioch.

"Belteshazzar came boldly before me and proved that his confidence was not misplaced. He recited both the dream and its interpretation. It was as though the God of Israel gave him total insight into my thoughts and dreams." Then the king called Daniel to join him on the dais. The king placed the robe he had been wearing upon the shoulders of Daniel, declaring, "Through Belteshazzar, I received the revelation of the mystery that had eluded all my counselors and me. With him as my advisor, I have access to the wisdom of the gods. The God of Belteshazzar is the one true God. He reveals mysteries that no man could possibly discern through his own wisdom."

"In accordance with the promises that I made to all my wise men, I am bestowing upon Belteshazzar great wealth and prestige. In addition, he is my chief counselor, the highest prefect in all of Babylon; he will be second in authority to me alone. If anyone fails to honor him or initiates any acts of treachery toward him, I will regard your treachery as an act of rebellion toward me. I will treat the matter as it deserves, so beware." The king gave Daniel one of the great houses of Babylon and many other gifts. He unstintingly fulfilled all his promises.

One of the first acts of Daniel in his new position was to speak to the king regarding the three of us. In some ways, I had become Daniel's right-hand man and most frequent companion, so I accompanied him before the king. "Your Highness possesses wisdom that exceeds the understanding of ordinary men as the brightness of the sun exceeds that of the moon. As you unquestionably understand, O king, I could never have interpreted your dream on my own. Had Adonai not revealed the dream to me, I would have been as helpless as the other men in your court. God revealed that dream in response to my prayers, but also in response to the prayers of Abed-nego, Shadrach, and Meshach. They're also dedicated servants of the Most High God and of you, Most Exalted King; therefore, they should share in the bounty that you're bestowing upon me."

The king looked at me and smiled. "Abed-nego, you're the son of Asher, the great warrior who resisted our advance into Jerusalem, are you not?"

"Yes, Your Highness, I'm his eldest son."

The king placed his right hand on my shoulder and declared, "The petition of Belteshazzar is right and good, as are all his words. Your loyalty to your God and to me will be rewarded. Though Belteshazzar will be the highest in the kingdom next to me, his three companions will be moved to positions of increased trust and importance. You'll soon be among the chief administrators of the province of Babylon. When you have matters of substantial concern or potential for good, you'll report to Belteshazzar, who shall be at my right hand within my court."

For several months, Hananiah, Mishael, and I lived with Daniel in the house that Nebuchadnezzar had given to him. It was one of the greatest houses in Babylon. Daniel remained a humble and unassuming man, so he was embarrassed by his riches and pleased to be able to share his home and bounty with us. However, over time, Daniel grew to be even more important to the realm. As the king interacted more closely with our leader, his wisdom and trustworthiness became more obvious. The king began to look to him in his everyday decisions, as well as the baffling mysteries. There was no one in the entire kingdom whose insight and discernment could compare with Daniel's or whose counsel the king valued half as much.

Though a foreigner and an exile from Jerusalem, Daniel's importance to the king increased over the next two years. Nebuchadnezzar needed and wanted Daniel even closer to him, so eventually, the king had Daniel move into his palace. We continued to live in Daniel's house. He would visit us when the king did not urgently require his counsel, but his visits became less frequent over time. As the confidence of Nebuchadnezzar in our leader increased, the king started sending Daniel to settle disputes in other realms of his kingdom. The king had always faced a dilemma. Though he did not trust his sages to handle foreign affairs, he had been reluctant to leave Babylon because of potential intrigue within his court. Daniel was his solution. The king knew that Daniel would wisely handle any disputes that arose in the conquered realms, no matter how sensitive the situation was. Daniel freed the king from having to leave Babylon.

Hananiah, Mishael, and I also distinguished ourselves in the administration to a lesser degree. We were punctual, honest, industrious, and even creative in our service to the king. In our personal lives, we continued to spend times exercising our devotion to Adonai, both individually and communally. We spurred one another to excel in our duties to the king by increasing out understanding of the culture and administration of the realm. Daniel kept track of our activities, regularly bringing them to the attention of the king. The result was steady promotion within the king's administration, much to the chagrin of our Chaldean colleagues. Within two years of interpreting the great dream, Daniel was securely established as the highest official in the court of Nebuchadnezzar, second in power only to the king. By that stage, Hananiah, Mishael, and I had also risen to positions of prominence, substantial trust, and power within the Chaldean court. The king had advanced us over the majority of Chaldeans in his court.

As is usually the case, such promotions unfailingly draw the attention of men. We came to feel the usual jealousy and resentment from those we passed over. These men had devoted their lives to the service of the realm. Though they were warm and respectful to our faces, many resented the authority that came with our advancement. Their disdain was not difficult to discern; those officials felt our ascension had come at their expense. They dismissed any possibility of merit on our part; they continually sought evidence to justify their scorn and soothe their bruised egos. They were convinced that our positions of prominence were merely the result of Daniel's patronage. In their eyes, there was nothing in our lives or work that justified our promotions. The satraps also resented Daniel—perhaps even more than they resented us—because he was over all the Chaldeans except Nebuchadnezzar. However, the king made his protection of Daniel clear to everyone. Our leader was far beyond their reach. We were not.

In a way, the resentment of the king's court toward us was ironic. If the quartet had not been in Babylon when the king had his dream, there was every reason to believe that all satraps and wise men in the Chaldean administration would have been executed. Nebuchadnezzar was not one to make idle threats. However, the intervention of Daniel, which resulted in the sparing of their lives, was conveniently forgotten within a few months of the event. Our roles were virtually unknown and completely unacknowledged. Given the opportunity, a large percentage of the administration would have done anything possible to bring Daniel down, but his position was unassailable. Moreover, our leader was careful and honest. He did nothing to open himself up to their venom. His antagonists may as well have set their target on the king. However, the three of us were within range of their wrath. Those over whom we had ascended started plotting against us shortly after we had achieved our positions of authority. They continually looked for ways to discredit us or completely remove us from their pathways to advancement. Though we were unaware of their venom, we were destined to feel its sting in the near future.

Even before the fateful dream, any objective observer of King Nebuchadnezzar would conclude that he had an enormous ego. It probably went with the position. Has there ever been a truly humble king? However, anyone seeking to measure the acme of the Chaldean monarch's ego would have all the information needed by reviewing Nebuchadnezzar's handling of the dream. Nebuchadnezzar was ready to execute all his counselors because they could not tell him the contents and interpretation of a dream which he had experienced but failed to recall; such an attitude reflects a seriously elevated sense of his own importance and the obligation of others toward him.

But if anything, Daniel's interpretation of the dream heightened the king's impression of his own worthiness; it seemed to confer a heavenly affirmation that he was the greatest king of all earthly realms. The dream was about kingdoms—the present realm and future kingdoms to come. The One True God had declared that Nebuchadnezzar was the head of gold, the most highly exalted portion of the statue. After hearing such a grandiose description of himself from the heavens, his ego demanded expression. In keeping with his generous nature, the king wanted all of Babylon to rejoice with him; he would give them the opportunity to show their obeisance and appreciation of his wondrous being.

The first step toward bringing his image into existence involved sending Daniel to Susa. Vital administrative issues suddenly arose in that volatile portion of the kingdom demanding immediate attention. The issues required a sensitive touch and understanding; Daniel was the only one who could do the job. Though my suspicions were never confirmed, I suspected the king wanted Daniel out of the way as his wondrous idol took shape. Without having to consult his second-in-command, Nebuchadnezzar understood how much his plans would conflict with the views of our leader. Almost as soon as Daniel left the palace, Nebuchadnezzar commissioned the construction of a great golden head that stood sixty cubits high, and it was six cubits across. The king had the idol constructed on the plain of Dura, which lies south of Babylon. As soon as the construction was underway in earnest, rumors and unofficial reports started circulating within the king's administration. All the satraps, prefects, governors, magistrates, and civil employees began discussing the details of the statue. Rumors circulated regarding an upcoming dedication for all to attend. The ceremony was to be grand. All were to come ready to show their obeisance to the image created by Nebuchadnezzar.

Hananiah, Mishael, and I got wind of the project. At work, we overheard the discussions between our comrades and their speculations about the details and purpose of the construction project. When we heard descriptions of the proposed idol, we decided that we needed to discuss the situation before receiving any official notification. Mishael said, "If what I hear in the scuttlebutt at work is anything close to the truth, this celebration of the king's statue clearly isn't going to be simple or voluntary. From the details that I've heard of this monstrosity, I think the king has constructed his portion of the statue from the dream. So when he has us all there for the dedication, it won't be for drinking tea and friendly banter. Unless I completely miss my guess, the dedication will be the king's summons for all his subjects to worship him through this statue that he's created. He'll expect everyone to honor his greatness, the head of the great statue from the dream. Does anyone see it differently?"

"Can there be any other interpretation? From the rumors I've heard, I draw the same conclusion. The idol almost exactly fits the image of our king described by Daniel in the dream," I replied. "Moreover, I get the impression the king won't take kindly to our opting out of his ceremony. How I wish we were in Susa with Daniel."

"Or he was here with us," opted Hananiah. "Somehow I don't think Nebuchadnezzar would force Daniel to worship his idol. Though this may border on blasphemy, I get the feeling that the king is somewhat in awe of our leader. Indeed, I think the urgent need for Daniel in Susa coincided too well with the construction plans of the king to be haphazard. Somehow, I don't think he regards us in the same manner; I don't expect him to treat us as he would treat Daniel. Indeed, I think he'll deal with us in a particularly unfriendly manner if we disappoint him."

"We should do everything possible to stay away from the plain of Dura and avoid contact with the king and his inner circle as preparations near completion. The best scenario would be that the entire ceremony goes on without us receiving an official notification. There'll be plenty of people there. The king will be in his moment. He'll be surrounded by dignitaries, so it's unlikely that he'd notice our absence," I added. "But the real question is what we will do if we are notified. If we cannot avoid the invitation, what are our options?"

Everyone went silent for a few moments. Then Hananiah said, "Do you really think it would be such a big deal." Mishael and I looked at him without comprehension, so he continued. "I completely agree with Azariah that the best thing for us to do is keep our heads down. What we want is to be able to avoid the summons and stay out of harm's way. We can all agree to that, but let's assume the invitation finds us. If everyone is required to bow down to this horrible idol on pain of death, do you really think that we should risk offending the king by obstinately defying his order? The idol is insentient, as we all understand, and the obeisance is just a onetime event. Would bowing the knee in response to an official declaration really affect our devotion to Adonai? Will that one show of obeisance undo our faithfulness?" Again, there was silence.

This time I broke the silence. "Yes." Then I paused before continuing, "Yes, I think it would be a big deal to show obeisance to that monstrosity—even once. Though I hope to avoid the conflict and have no desire to infuriate the king, I can't and won't bow down to that idol even if we're forced to attend the ceremony. I will not presume to answer for the two of you. You must settle the question in your own hearts, but I think of my father facing the battle against the Chaldeans. Our nation was in trouble because King Jehoiakim foolishly withheld the tribute from Nebuchadnezzar. Abba seemed to understand, even then, that he would be the one sent to delay the Chaldeans' charge. He knew that he was likely to die defending our land. He did what he had to as unto the Lord because he knew it was the right thing to do. In his last words to me, he urged me to be a man of faith and courage. When I consider the situation that Abba faced, I believe that he would have avoided the battle if he could do do by any legitimate means; if he could've by-passed the fight without impugning his faith and courage."

"In the same vein, I think we're right to seek to avoid a showdown with Nebuchadnezzar. I'll take any steps I can to avoid the invitation from the king, but if I'm forced to go to the plain of Dura, I cannot bow my knees before that hideous idol. If my father could face death while seeking to right the errors of a foolish king, I must do my duty, even if it comes because of an arrogant king's ego. I'll refuse to bow. I will stand my ground and bear whatever consequences Nebuchadnezzar brings upon me. In truth, I feel that I cannot choose otherwise."

Initially my friends just stared at me, as though trying to comprehend my true meaning.

Quietly but firmly, Mishael said, "Of course, you're right. Though I wish I could find fault with your logic, you've made the issue a matter of faith and honor. Viewed from that perspective, I have to agree with your conclusion. If we can legitimately avoid the invitation and stay away from the plain of Dura, it's the appropriate thing for us to do, but if the king forces a standoff, I'm with you, Azariah. I can't and won't bow down to that monstrosity."

"Then it's settled," replied Hananiah. "If we can avoid trouble, we will, but if the king forces us to either bow down to his idol or die, we stand together and accept the consequences. God protected us before when Nebuchadnezzar was going to kill all the educated men in Babylon. He revealed the king's dream to Daniel in a miraculous way. Perhaps God will intervene for us again, even at the last moment. But whether he does or not, we stand firm in our faith. We won't be intimidated by the king. We won't show obeisance to the false god."

The discussion that evening was the most critical event in each of our lives. Our subsequent obedience flowed out of that discussion and the vows that we made to God and one another. Our leader was not with us in person, but we all knew how he would have responded. A solemn bond was formed that night. Nothing more was said. Nothing more was needed.

After coming to our joint resolution, we all wanted to reduce the tension and engage in some lighter conversation, but the mood was too heavy, somber, intense for banter. We had no desire to dwell on the forthcoming conflict or discuss the matter any further. We had come to our joint resolution. The atmosphere was too charged for any other discussion, so we remained silent. We had come to our decision before the Lord and one another. Each of us knew that he would abide by his decision and that his companions would stand with him. Though we would diligently seek to avoid the contact that would make attending the ceremony mandatory, I think we all knew that our Chaldean colleagues would make sure that the summons reached us. In the depth of our souls, we all understood that we were going to have the opportunity to make our professions good.

CHAPTER FOUR

Taking a Stance

OUR HACKLES WERE UP AFTER OUR PRIVATE COUNCIL, BUT the next few weeks made me wonder if perhaps our intense conference had been unnecessary. When the rumors started flowing regarding the idol and the anticipated demands that the king would impose, several Chaldeans sought to precipitate a reaction from me by making comments about the upcoming ceremony. Sensing their impertinence and understanding their goal, I acted nonchalant and noncommittal. When I was forced to speak, I tried to convince them that whatever Nebuchadnezzar was doing was of no interest to me.

Bigthan, an administrator over whom I had ascended, seemed to be the leader of a group of coworkers who sought to irritate and get a reaction from me. "Abed-nego, isn't this a wonderful time to be alive and in Babylon? We're sure you must be as excited as we are about the statue that the king is constructing. Aren't you simply bubbling over as you prepare to join us in making obeisance to this image that the gods have given us through our king?"

Though I perfectly comprehended both his meaning and intentions, I looked at him quizzically and replied, "In truth, I haven't given the matter much thought. I don't usually get caught up in unsubstantiated rumors. Since the king has made no official announcement, I presume the story about some wondrous statue being constructed is just another idle rumor spread by the bored and ignorant." Several of his colleagues snickered at my retort. After multiple attempts failed to elicit an angry response from me, they eventually tired of their game.

The construction of the idol was delayed for numerous technical reasons, none of which interested me. My colleagues at work had nothing to say to me during that time, as they had given up their attempts to raise my ire. Though I could not be certain, it seemed to me that my subordinates were watching me more carefully than they had before. Hananiah and Mishael had the same feeling at their places of work, but during the three weeks that followed those initial rumors, we heard nothing. Whatever Nebuchadnezzar was doing on the Dura plain, he seemed to keep his own counsel.

Just when I started to feel that we had worried in vain, Arioch came to my workplace. By all I could tell, Arioch seemed to like and respect us, but it also seemed that this captain of the king's bodyguard was the designated bearer of bad news, at least for us. The three of us were working in different areas, but Arioch came to each place and read the following proclamation.

> To: The citizens of Babylon, the rulers and satraps of the realm, all wise men, and counselors of King Nebuchadnezzar
>
> From: His Sovereign Majesty
>
> Rejoice with me, my loyal subjects. Our long wait is over and will soon yield great benefits. The gods have finally made clear to me the design of an image that is both worthy of the heavens and appropriate for our earthly realm. After prolonged prayer and meditation, the gods laid on my heart the perfect plans for the image to represent the gods to our people. We have all been counting the days until the unveiling. I am proud to announce that the construction of that image has at last been completed.

In three days, all subjects of my realm and in particular, the appointed rulers, satraps, and leaders of our people shall gather on the plain of Dura and pay homage to the image that the gods have given us. When the great statue is unveiled, the trumpets will blast and be joined by the horns, lyre, zither, bagpipes, and other musical instruments as they call us to worship. When you hear that musical interlude, you will have the privilege of showing your obeisance to this great image of the gods by falling on your faces in worship of the statue. Anyone failing to attend the unveiling or refusing to bow down to the image shall forfeit his life in a most horrible fashion. He shall be cast into the furnace of the king and therein be consumed. Take heed, all my citizens, for my word has been spoken. There will be no exceptions.

Nebuchadnezzar
The Great King of the Chaldeans

Our hopes of avoiding the summons vanished with the announcement. Even as Arioch was reading, I glanced around and noted several subordinates who seemed to pay inordinate attention to my reaction, so I steeled my countenance. I refused to react to the announcement or acknowledge their impertinence. Though I did everything in my power not to give them the pleasure of seeing how unwelcome the reading was, Arioch's announcement felt like a blow to the gut.

That evening we convened for another council. "Our hope of avoiding the summons has failed," I said gloomily. "Arioch looked directly at me as he read the invitation. I'm sure that he did the same with each of you. Moreover, several colleagues in my workplace took on the appearance of vultures as he read; they eyed me as if I were a wounded beast. The possibility that we'll be able to avoid the unveiling or detection when we refuse to bow down at the king's command is virtually nil. Though I won't try to hold either of you to your previous vows, I'm still committed to standing against the king's edict. When the caravan is organized, I'll go to the plain of Dura, for I think that's unavoidable, but when the horn blows, I won't bow. Perhaps Adonai will cause our rebellion to go unnoticed, but whatever his good pleasure is, I cannot change. I will remain vertical."

Hananiah replied, "We've been through this. My decision was made weeks ago. It hasn't and won't change."

"Nor mine," declared Mishael with resolution in his mien and voice.

I looked at my two colleagues and smiled. "You two make me proud. You're like King Josiah, our faithful king who came from a family that was dominated by apostates. You're as firm as that great king in your devotion to God. Since our arrival in Babylon, it's been my privilege to be your friend. If this event is to be our death, as all indications seem to suggest, it'll be an honor to die with you." They responded to me in kind.

The following day, a caravan for the leaders of the Chaldean people was formed, and the three of us were installed as a central cog in the march to Dura. Like most cities, Babylon is built on the crest of several hills near a river. The plain of Dura is a wide and fertile land, which stretches from Babylon down to the Euphrates River. It is some of the most fertile, productive land in the Chaldean Empire.

It was the season for planting. Those who tilled the land and planted were afield, busily engaged in their critically important work of preparing their fields to catch the early rains. Families of all ages were engaged in the work that would supply their food for the upcoming year. They seemed untroubled by the king's announcement, and I envied them. I had no idea whether or not they would be joining us before the king's idol. Their issue was preparing for the crops that they needed for survival. Though some of the people clearly lived on the plain, it appeared to me that the majority of the people were from Babylon because there were far more people laboring in the field than there were homes to accommodate them.

We reached the site of the monstrosity early in the evening. That night, we slept under the stars, for the weather was mild. The three of us were separate from the rest, but that was so common that it struck no one as strange or inappropriate. We prayed together. Our most frequently repeated prayer was that the Lord would give us the courage to stand firm in the struggle that we would face on the following day. Our most persistent requests were that Adonai would protect our souls and that he would be honored by our dedication. Then we hugged one another and repeated our vow to stand firm.

Toward the end of twilight, Bigthan came to us. "Well, Shadrach, Meshach, and Abed-Nego, are the three of you excited about tomorrow? It seems like a big day for everyone, but especially for you three. I'm only sorry your friend Belteshazzar won't be here to join in the celebration. In case any of you have doubts, let me assure you that all your friends and colleagues will be watching you closely tomorrow. We're all ready to report to the king regarding your exemplary behavior as you demonstrate your sincere obeisance."

Bigthan was a heavyset man who probably would have been tall had he not been so stooped over. Because of his posture, the bald crown of his head was his most visible feature. He never looked us in the face during either the earlier encounters or this harangue. But toward the end of his snide remarks, he did elevate his left eye sufficiently to glance at our necks. He had a leering grin that we could barely see, but we heard his raspy, evil laugh as he took his leave. I looked around and noted numerous malignant stares from other colleagues, but Bigthan was the only one who was impertinent enough to actually mock our distress. Again, we steeled ourselves against any reaction to his harangue and remained mute. They would get no satisfaction from us.

Despite the looming showdown, the palpable hatred of the colleagues in our caravan, and the rocky ground of the plain of Dura, the three of us slept surprisingly soundly that night. The next morning the malignant and contemptuous stares from the night before were even more prominent. Our enemies could barely contain their glee, for they felt that they had us in a vice. Either we would compromise our beliefs, or we would die. Though I was sure that their greater desire was to hear of our final removal from Nebuchadnezzar's hierarchy, I believed that hearing reports of our compromise would have satisfied them. What they really wanted were the grounds to despise us. They longed to add evidence to their belief that we were cowards and did not deserve our positions or authority. They sought to justify the disdain that they felt for us. They felt that they could not lose that day because the scenario before us seemed to allow for only two conclusions: our deaths or the show of cowardice and inconsistency. Either one would have satisfied them.

The three of us broke the fast together and set out with the group for the place of dedication. As we walked toward the site, we prayed for courage and faith. Then we took our places among our colleagues. The king and his entourage arrived by the second hour, and the plain of Dura was packed with the king's subjects and various dignitaries. Interminable speeches were given, celebrating the greatness of the king, the wonder of the great image that the gods had revealed to Nebuchadnezzar, and the tremendous opportunity that they had to worship this gift now that it had been so wonderfully constructed under the king's directions.

At about the fifth hour, the stiflingly boring preliminaries were completed. It was time for the great unveiling. Though I noticed that Bigthan and his colleagues had had their eyes on us intermittently throughout the ceremony, at the conclusion of the speeches, it seemed as if all eyes locked on us. Suddenly the trumpets sounded. They were joined by a cacophony of other musical instruments. The musical interlude preceded the dropping of the cloth, which revealed the hideous idol. As the cloth fell to the ground, so did every man, woman, and child on the plain of Dura that day—everyone but the three of us. Even the king and all his dignitaries prostrated themselves before the idol. After everyone had remained in the position of obeisance for approximately five minutes, the crier sent out his message freeing everyone to arise. Hananiah, Mishael, and I simply walked away from the site of dedication without looking at anyone. However, none of us had any thought that we had escaped notice. In that, we were soon confirmed.

CHAPTER FIVE

Facing the Fire

THREE HOURS AFTER THE CEREMONY ENDED, THE THREE of us arrived in Babylon. We sat together at Daniel's home in a state of high agitation. We had taken the stance that we had agreed upon. We knew what lay ahead. As we awaited the consequences, we were not in the mood for banter. Though we were sorely tempted to try to escape and seek some place of refuge until the event was at least a bit more distant in the king's mind, we knew that flight was impossible. Even a delay in reaping the wrath of Nebuchadnezzar was unattainable. Bigthan and his cronies would be watching our every move and would spoil any attempt to escape. Though we knew what lay ahead, none of us expressed any regret.

I finally broke the silence by remarking, "Well, our path is established. Since I don't regret our decision to defy the king's edict, it would be insane to stew over our predicament. What I'd like to say is how proud I was to stand together with you two in defiance of the king's outrageous demands. Though this will probably lead to my death, I am still pleased with our resolve. I'm proud that we refused to compromise. I cannot imagine any other companions with whom I would rather face death. If I have any regrets, it's that I didn't have the chance to know you better in Jerusalem and that our years together in Babylon have been few. Whether we die now or in fourscore more years, I will always be proud to be your friend."

Both Hananiah and Mishael expressed similar feelings. After a lull in the conversation, Hananiah asked, "What will we do if Nebuchadnezzar gives us the option to repent and bow down to the idol?"

"The offer wouldn't tempt me in the least," I replied with no hesitation. "Indeed, I'd feel more foolish bowing down now than if I had joined all the others in their obeisance. Again, that is my decision and not necessarily yours, but if we're pressured into submitting, the king will have turned our initial defiance into a farce. Bowing down at this point would make me feel ridiculous as well as faithless. To me, it would have been better to have bowed with everyone else than to be pressured into doing it at this time."

Hananiah's face registered some pain and indecision as I spoke, but Mishael responded decisively. "I'm in total agreement. This is the time to show our mettle. Your father's a hero in my mind. I'm convinced that many in Jerusalem feel the same way about him. Perhaps they'll feel the same way about us if word of our defying the king's edict gets out, although I doubt any of our Chaldean friends will send a favorable report about us to Jerusalem."

"And perhaps Adonai will intervene for us," added Hananiah, "but whatever happens, I'm firm. If we die today, we'll be with the Lord and your father. If we're given a second chance, we'll decline it immediately. Though I raised the question, I'm not faltering. I'm with you."

The words of Hananiah still hung in the air when there was a rap on the door, and Arioch entered our dwelling. Though he had always been friendly toward us in the past, his face was stern, and he studiously avoided eye contact with each of us. He unrolled a decree and read it before us (in Chaldean, of course).

> Shadrach, Meshach, and Abed-Nego, satraps who are in positions of high honor because of the graciousness of King Nebuchadnezzar: you are commanded to appear before your sovereign and give answers to reports of your rebellion and defiance against your king. Furthermore, you are commanded to come immediately before the

great throne of Nebuchadnezzar and if possible, give
a suitable explanation to the charges upon your heads.

With that, Arioch rolled up the parchment and spoke to us. He
shook his head and asked, "What were the three of you thinking when
you defied the king's edict? Are you insane? Never have I seen our king
as enraged as when Bigthan reported your defiance and refusal to bow
to the king's statue. Personally, I have a great regard for each of you.
I believe that you have been and can continue to be strongly positive
influences in our land and culture, but to do that, you must submit to
the king and pay homage to his statue today. Everyone understands that
you reserve your true worship for the Hebrew God, but I advise you
to put that aside for a time and go through the motions of obeisance
to the king's idol. If you continue in your refusal to bow to the king's
idol, you'll die today. There's no possibility that he'll be lenient with
you. Consider carefully as we travel, for as soon as we arrive, you'll go
immediately before the king, and this matter will be settled today, one
way or the other."

The words of Arioch were expected, but they cast a pall over
me, so I glanced over at my companions. The color had drained
from their countenances to some degree, but there was no hint of
indecision. Though I had expressed my admiration for them earlier,
I felt it even more than I had before. I was proud to face death with
such men. How could anyone have better companions when heading
into mortal combat?

When we arrived before the throne of the king, he was pacing
and gesticulating wildly. His face was flushed. He was speaking and
muttering to himself. He turned upon us like a wolf ready to pounce
upon its prey. "What is this that I've heard? Surely, the stories must be
false. It cannot possibly be true that men I've treated so well, advanced
over my own countrymen, and placed in such positions of trust would
turn against me. How could you refuse to pay homage to the great
image that was delivered to me by the wisdom of the gods? There
must be a mistake. Perhaps you were confused. I'm prepared to give
you another opportunity to repent of the ingratitude that you have
shown me. My officials and I will accompany you back to the plain of

Dura and give you a second chance to redeem your error. The music will sound again just as before. If you fall down and worship the great statue, all will be forgiven. However, if you refuse, you'll be cast into the great furnace that you see before you. What god can protect you from that agonizing death?"

At the conclusion of the king's harangue, I stepped forward. "Oh, great king, though we mean no defiance or disrespect to you, our primary allegiance is to another. We worship Adonai, the God of Israel. We cannot show obeisance to an idol as though there was another deity that is equal to the One True God in heaven. We do not need another opportunity to prove our resolve to you. If you march us out to that plain and the music sounds, we'll still refuse to bow down and pay homage to your pagan image. We'll continue to worship the One True God only. Adonai is able to keep us safe, even in your furnace if he so chooses. But even if he does not, we choose death rather than worship the false god you've created. That is our stance. May God help us."

Though the visage of the king was altered more than I had ever seen it, his countenance became even more twisted and contorted with rage. "Increase the heat of the furnace. Make it far hotter than we've ever experienced. Make it seven times hotter than usual." Then muttering to himself, he said, "Defy me, will they? We'll see what god is able to protect them from me."

When the king in his anger ordered the stoking of the furnace, he gave us a momentary reprieve. Without even realizing it, we had turned toward one another, and we were holding hands. Mishael whispered to me, "Well said. Your father must be proud as he looks down upon us today. You succinctly expressed just what I feel. I only wish there was someone here who could record your words and tell them to our fellow countrymen. As you said earlier, I couldn't choose companions with whom I'd rather face death." Hananiah nodded in agreement.

As the servants gathered wood and charcoal to stoke up the furnace, Arioch came over to us. "Well, you have my admiration as well as my condolences. You lads are certainly brave, even if you're completely deranged. We have a few minutes. As you can clearly see, there's no possibility that the king will alter his decree, but if you cast yourselves at his feet and vow to do as he commands, I believe that even now he'll allow you to submit. You can live to face another day if you'll humble yourselves before him."

Hananiah said, "Thank you, Arioch. You've been good to us since our arrival in Babylon. We understand and appreciate your concern, but we cannot change. Take heart. We believe Adonai will intervene for us even at this late hour."

Even though it was far from his intended result, the order to super heat the furnace caused a delay of almost an hour as the king's servants gathered the fuel and stoked the flames. The king never once looked over at us during that interval, but his mutterings and gesticulations increased as time went by. I wondered if he was thinking about Daniel and reviewing our roles in the interpretation of his enigmatic dream. Though I sensed that he was torn, even sad that he was forced to continue with the sentence that he had pronounced, I believe that he felt he could not relent at that stage of the proceedings. During the interval, we were praying and encouraging one another with our bond of friendship and devotion to Adonai. Though we were still looking to God to intervene on our behalves, each of us knew that any rescue was virtually impossible.

When Arioch reported to the king that the furnace had reached the desired heat, the king commanded in a subdued voice, "Bind them. Cast them into the furnace." Strong hands laid hold of us and ripped us apart from one another. Our hands and feet were bound. The door to the furnace was pried open, and a blast of hot air hit us as we were hurdled into the flame.

CHAPTER SIX

Meeting a Fourth

A S WE HAD WAITED FOR THE FURNACE TO HEAT UP, IT HAD occurred to me that the king's attempt to wreak greater vengeance upon us by super heating the furnace would only make our deaths that much quicker and therefore, less painful. But it was not to be. I landed on my feet and seemed to be dreaming. Instead of excruciating pain and death, the flames did nothing unpleasant or unwelcome. The ropes that had been tied on my hands and feet burned immediately—even before I reached the floor of the furnace—so I did not even fall. The fears that had crowded into my mind as we had waited proved groundless. Instead of pain or death, I felt an overwhelming sense of contentment and well-being.

As I looked over at Hananiah and Mishael, I was surprised to see another with us. Hananiah and Mishael were looking at him as well. Though he had a form like us, he was completely different from us. We needed no trumpets to prompt us to fall before the Great One, but he raised us up and hugged each of us. Then he bent down and removed the vestiges of rope that were clinging to our wrists and ankles.

How long were we in the furnace having fellowship with the Great One? I have no ability to estimate. It seemed like an eternity, and it seemed like seconds. We communed with the Great One, and he ministered to us. We talked, laughed, and enjoyed being in one another's presence. What did we talk about? Perhaps I should be ashamed to admit it, but I truly cannot recall his exact words. He conveyed his pleasure that we had trusted him and resisted the temptation to compromise, but primarily, he let us know how much it pleased him to be with us. Our session was a time for communion and not instruction. His words were friendly, profound, loving, and encouraging. He taught my soul necessary truths, but the intimacy we experienced was far greater and more important than any information that I received from that conversation. Any knowledge that he conveyed was of secondary importance. He clearly shared with us essential truths that our hearts needed and yearned to hear about his love, paternal pride, pleasure in our company, and longing for the time when our fellowship would never be broken. It was a wondrous time. Later, I wished that I could revisit that furnace. I never wanted it to end.

We had been through many horrible experiences over the last month. For weeks, we lived through anxious moments of dread as we considered the plans of Nebuchadnezzar and the idol that he was constructing. Every day, we had to endure the sneering arrogance of our coworkers as they contemplated either our cowardice or demise. Our hearts were heavy as Arioch read the sentence of condemnation to us. The furious visage of the great king almost took our breaths away when we were ushered into his presence. We experienced the zenith of our fears when we were jerked asunder and bound so that we could be cast into the furnace. However, the worst thing that happened to us during that entire period was when the furnace cooled down, the door was opened, and the Great One departed. His exit caused each of us to grieve viscerally. I am convinced that we will one day be with the Great One again. That assurance is the greatest anticipation of my life.

When the door of the furnace opened, Nebuchadnezzar called out to us, "Shadrach, Meshach, and Abed-Nego, servants of the Most High God, come out of the furnace." After we looked around and confirmed that the Great One was gone, we obeyed the king. With the Great One's departure, we had no reason or desire to stay in the furnace. As we exited, those who had been in attendance to the king gawked at us. Several reached out to touch us. Over to the side, I saw the lifeless bodies of the men who had thrown us into the furnace. They had been killed when the blast of extreme heat hit them, as the furnace door was pried open. I looked at my companions and was surprised to see that their clothing and hair was unharmed. When I smelled my clothes, there was not even a trace of smoky odor upon them.

Arioch sidled up to me and asked, "Who was the fourth one with you in the furnace?"

I replied, "Though I don't know who he was, he was certainly a wondrous being. Was he God? Clearly, he was sent from God. Perhaps he was God in human form."

Arioch nodded. "I think he must have been a god."

Then the king declared before all the officials who were present, "Blessed be the God of Shadrach, Meshach, and Abed-Nego, for he is the One True God. He has protected the lives of these three brave men from my wrath. No other deity could have spared them in my furnace. There is no other deity in heaven or on earth that rivals the power of Israel's God. These young men were fearless. They boldly defied my orders and yielded up their bodies in service to the One True God. Their lives were precious in his sight today. From this day forward, if anyone speaks offensively or disrespectfully of the God of Israel—the God of Shadrach, Meshach, and Abed-Nego—he and his family shall die, and his possessions shall be destroyed. There is no other god in all the heavens who is like the God of Israel." Then the king rose from his throne, embraced each of us, and honored us in much the same way that he had honored our friend Daniel.

Book Two
THE RESTORATION

P ROLOGUE. AFTER BEING FORCIBLY EXILED TO BABYLON, Daniel, Azariah, Hananiah, and Mishael were confronted with challenging and potentially mortal adventures. Their early adventures were narrated in Book 1, *The Furnace*. They were threatened with death because Nebuchadnezzar had a dream that he could not remember, but Adonai revealed the dream and the interpretation to Daniel. The book ended as Azariah, Hananiah, and Mishael were threatened with death unless they paid obeisance to Nebuchadnezzar's idol. Despite being pelted with the logical persuasions to compromise, they remained faithful to Adonai and refused to bow before the idol. They experienced the faithfulness of Adonai and survived the Chaldean king's furnace. Book 2 begins in the aftermath of that adventure. As our story resumes, the Babylonian quartet have achieved positions of some authority within the court of Nebuchadnezzar, the great Chaldean king, but they were still young men in a foreign culture with many adventures ahead. Azariah (Abed-Nego) continues to narrate the story.

CHAPTER SEVEN

Personal Matters

I BELIEVE THAT EVERY MAN TORTURES HIMSELF WITH ONE OF the most basic questions of life. How will he fare when faced with the great challenges that life imposes? Does he have the essential qualities of manhood? Men are raised with certain expectations from their fathers, brothers, friends, and themselves. We have an unexpressed uncertainty about our souls, hearts, characters. We are haunted by a deep-seated fear that when the time of testing comes, we will fail; we will be proven cowards who are inadequate to don the mantle of manhood. We are worried that we will disappoint our fathers, our brothers, ourselves. Perhaps, this is our greatest fear. We grow in our beliefs. We seek to obtain courage and long to prepare ourselves for the great challenge and the defining moment in our lives. We want to be assured that we will stay firm to our course when put to the test.

When Abba saw the hordes of Chaldeans approaching Jerusalem, he knew that his moment had come. He comported himself well. In the time before his commissioning and during the battle itself, Abba showed himself to be a man of courage and faith, even though the defining moment of his life resulted in his death. But as I mourned for Abba, I was also envious. He had proven himself at the time of his great trial. It was far better to stand firm and die than to give in to fears and live with a hollow chest. How horrible it would be to walk away from the challenge with the realization that the better part of your soul had already withered away and was simply waiting for the body to follow and find a home in Sheol.

Our trio—Hananiah, Mishael, and I—had experienced our moment of testing. While Daniel, our leader, was away in Susa, King Nebuchadnezzar built a golden idol as a tribute to himself. He sought to force our obeisance. Everyone on the plain of Dura that day fell in worship of the idol, but the three of us stood in defiance of the king's order. When offered a second opportunity to avoid Nebuchadnezzar's fiery furnace, we stood together as brothers who trusted Adonai. Though we were willing to die rather than comply with the king's orders, the Lord spared our lives when we were cast into the furnace. The Lord met us in a way that we had never known before. No one needed a sharper challenge than we had faced. Each of us was proud of the way that we fared. Of course, we were thrilled to have been spared in such a dramatic fashion; we could speak of nothing else for a day or so, but afterward, our joy became more visceral and personal. After those first couple of days, the event was never mentioned. Never again did we need to say anything to each other or anyone else about that time and challenge. We knew. Each of us had faced the test. With each other's support, we had passed.

Before we had been cast into the fire, the temptation to compromise, bow our knees just that one time, to accept Nebuchadnezzar's offer for a second chance was keenly felt by each of us. By the grace of God and the comradery of our brothers, we resisted. We stood together and strengthened one another in our resolve as we looked to Adonai. Our time of testing had come, but unlike my father, we had survived our great challenge. We had defied the king's order and remained faithful to our God. Adonai intervened to spare our lives. To have faced death without flinching and been spared in such a miraculous way was the most exhilarating experience of my young life. My courage had been sufficient for that trial. That experience gave me confidence as I looked to the future.

The next challenge was to return to the routine of life. One trial was returning to a workplace filled with men who hated me without cause, except for jealousy and possibly prejudice against my race. Without question, I knew these men had done everything that they could to bring about my death. They had rejoiced as they informed the king of our defiance. They were jovial when they considered our imminent demise. Arioch had mentioned that Bigthan had been the one reporting to the king. Nebuchadnezzar did not single out any of the other conspirators, but I knew that many in our workplace shared Bigthan's desire to see me perish. Now they were justifiably afraid of me. Though I had no desire to increase their dread, I did not intend to lessen their fears. One of the most pleasant fruits of the entire episode was that those who hated me so vehemently made it a practice to stay out of my way. Indeed, about the only interactions that I had with them for months were when they sought to appease me by doing little favors and showing other signs of obeisance. Hananiah and Mishael told me that they had similar experiences in their areas of work.

In our desire to honor God, we continued the work before us. We sought to treat all our subordinates and coworkers decently. We acted as though we were unaware of the hatred that they had demonstrated and the steps that they had taken against us. I acted that way even toward Bigthan. However, I never said anything to him to lessen his fear of me. I was pleased that he avoided me as much as possible. I never again had to endure his condescending smirk or evil laugh.

Our quartet had been among the first group of exiles that had been transported from Jerusalem to Babylon, but many more followed as the years rolled by and the troubles in Jerusalem continued to escalate. Small groups of Jewish exiles came to the Chaldean capital regularly. The number of people leaving Jerusalem increased exponentially as King Zedekiah, the brother of the displaced King Jehoiakim, started making more of the same insane decisions that predecessor had made.

Part of my administrative duty evolved into meeting the exiles who were coming into Babylon. It was my responsibility to assist them during their transition, an assignment I relished. Following our episode in the furnace when I had been high in the king's favor, I had petitioned him for this position. King Nebuchadnezzar was a despot, as he had proven time and time again, but he was wise in many of his decisions. Instead of annihilating the wisest and strongest of his vanquished opponents, he incorporated them into the Chaldean culture. Our quartet was evidence of the wisdom of such an approach, and Nebuchadnezzar extended it to others. When the Jewish people who fled the disastrous regime in Jerusalem came to Babylon, they were treated with respect. They were given the opportunity and tools to settle into Chaldean society. The king truly wanted our people to succeed and become fruitful members of his realm. My responsibility was to greet them, convince them of Nebuchadnezzar's desire to see them succeed, and make sure that the proper assistance was available to help them make the transition.

All the exiles were traumatized when they arrived in Babylon, a land that I had come increasingly to identify as my own. The newly arrived exiles needed reassurance of their welcome into the land and specific guidance about their next steps. They also had significant practical needs. They needed land, tools, and seeds for cultivation. They were desperate to find friends and colleagues with whom they could talk and confide in during this harrowing period of transition. They longed for encouragement from those who had been through the ordeal so that they, too, would know that they could survive. I had a large staff, which included many people from Judah and other conquered lands; I had trained workers from all the conquered realms to assist those who were coming in and took an active role in the process, particularly among the Jews.

About a year after my ordeal with the furnace, a large group from Jerusalem arrived. As I surveyed the traumatized exiles, I was shocked and thrilled to find the remnants of my family. My mother had grayed substantially in the ten years since Abba's death and my abduction, but she still impressed me with her strength and determination. Simeon, the second child, was now a man, but those years in Jerusalem as the head of the family appeared to have taken their toll. He must have borne most of my family's burden. The stigma of suffering was apparent in his countenance as well as in his stooped appearance. Still, I read in his mien a quiet joy that he had arrived and a determination to succeed. He was thrilled to find me, as were all my family members. We were fortunate in that only one of my siblings had died during the horrendous years in Jerusalem. My family fared better than most. In addition, Elizabeth, the third-born child and oldest girl, was a widow with two children. Her husband had died two years earlier from the dysentery that had swept through the city during the first few months of Nebuchadnezzar's siege of Jerusalem.

Initially, all of my family came to live in my home. Like all the exiles upon arriving, each family member received tools, a parcel of land, and seeds for planting. I encouraged them to utilize what they had received. Though I was in a position to liberally supplement their finances, and I offered some of my own land for cultivation if they needed more, I wanted to see them provide for themselves. As I had observed many times, the exiles who did well were those who were determined to exert themselves, start again, plant roots in Babylon, and regain control of their lives. My own family members needed to take steps to recover. They needed to play an active role in their own resettlement. After they had exerted themselves, they could take pride in making the transition. My brothers had brought a few sheep and goats, which were the minuscule surviving remnant of our flocks. I put them in a pasture with my own flocks, which was something that I generally did not offer to most of the exiles.

Though I was not cognizant of it until later, it gradually dawned on me that God had enabled me to fulfill the charge that my father had put on me. As he left for his battle, Abba transferred the mantle of providing for the family to me. Nebuchadnezzar had made sure that my family had been given sufficient food because of my role in his court. But in this more critical situation when their needs were at their zenith, Adonai had placed me in a position to meet their needs more palpably. God had put me in a position that was similar to our patriarch Joseph. Just as Joseph went before his family and facilitated their transition to a foreign land, I went before my mother and siblings into Babylon and provided for them in their transition. Eventually all my family members moved out on their own, except my mother, who stayed with me until I was transferred to Susa many years later. Elizabeth, my widowed sister, and her children stayed with me for two years, but she ended up remarrying. Though I never knew her first husband, I strongly approved of her second spouse.

In the second year of overseeing the welcoming of exiles, a woman from Jerusalem handed me a letter from the prophet Jeremiah. Because I remembered Abba speaking favorably about Jeremiah when I had been a lad, I was intimidated as I opened the letter. It was incumbent upon me to follow the directions of this true prophet of God. However, I was unsure of how he would look upon the loyalty that our quartet had developed for the Chaldean king. I wondered what I would do if Jeremiah called upon God's people to rebel against Nebuchadnezzar.

However, my misgivings were groundless. Through Jeremiah, God instructed his people to assimilate into the Chaldean culture. Though Adonai plainly told the exiles that there would be no quick solutions or immediate return to Jerusalem, God assured the people of his love for them. The Lord told us that his plans for us were for our good and not our calamity. He would be with us. He would give us a future and a hope. No, we would not return to Jerusalem, but our children would. Adonai gave us his promise that our people would once again inhabit Jerusalem, but for the next seventy years, we would be in exile. He encouraged his people to settle into the land, marry, build houses, work, be productive, and become vital parts of the Chaldean culture. After we had been in exile for seventy years, he would bring our children back.

Because the king was appropriately careful about outside influences, I took the letter to Nebuchadnezzar for his perusal. As I expected, he enthusiastically endorsed the reading of the letter to the Jews coming into exile. Therefore, in addition to speaking on behalf of King Nebuchadnezzar to each new group that arrived from Judea, welcoming them, and encouraging them to make Babylon their new home, I read Jeremiah's letter, which exhorted the people to resettle in Babylon as a demonstration of their faith in Adonai. I believe that the encouragement from Jeremiah's letter was a great boost to them in the transition.

It was in this capacity of welcoming exiles that the trajectory of my life changed. As I addressed a new group of refugees just arriving from Jerusalem, I recognized more familiar faces. It pleased me to see that my father's cousin was among the group. Abba and Isaac had been close in their adolescence and our families had continued to have significant interactions in the years before Abba's death. Like my father, Isaac was a shepherd. He had brought the remnant of his herd with him. Their numbers had been decimated when King Zedekiah rebelled against the Chaldeans. The herds had declined even more substantially as starvation, disease, and other torturous aspects of the siege bore their wonted effects.

After I had helped the rest of the people, I invited Isaac and his family to stay in my home as they worked through their transition, just as I had done with my own family. Moreover, I assured him that I had sufficient pastureland where he could graze his remaining livestock. Isaac had brought all his remaining family with him. His wife had died in the pestilence that had been introduced by the siege, as had a daughter and two sons. But he had eight children, one daughter-in-law, two sons-in-law, and six grandchildren. Mama, Elizabeth, and her children were still with me, but, with a few adjustments, my home could accommodate them and the new family. Isaac had been one of Abba's closest friends. He was on good terms with my mother. The welcome that she extended was genuine and heartfelt. My home initially felt squeezed for a bit, but as we all settled into a routine, we adjusted and were comfortable.

After taking the family members to the house, I turned them over to Elizabeth. She was sufficiently settled to find space for our cousins and help them feel at home; I went out to show the shepherd the fields. My plans were to instruct him where he could take their flocks, point out places for both watering and grazing, and to warn him about some of the hazards of the area where several of our sheep had been injured over the years. My grazing land was well watered, and the grasses were abundant, so I knew that in at least one needful area, my assistance would be welcomed by Isaac.

To my surprise, the shepherd was a young woman. Rachel was Isaac's youngest child. Since she was a cousin, I was sure that we had met at some point in our lives, but she would have been quite young when I was taken away. She was no longer a little girl and nothing like I remembered her. Rachel was seventeen, modest, and beautifully formed. She was somewhat tall and unconsciously graceful. She had wavy black hair that extended midway down her back. When she got over her shyness, I had the chance to gaze into her eyes and upon her physiognomy; I was utterly enchanted. She had strong, dark brown eyes, which promised intelligence and depth of character. She had high cheekbones and a jaw that was strong yet feminine. Her lips puckered slightly forming an archer's bow. When she smiled, her entire countenance lit up like a lantern, dispersing a glow on all around. There were beautiful women in

Nebuchadnezzar's court as well as scattered throughout Babylon, but to my eyes, none could compare with Rachel. I was smitten from the start.

When I escorted her out to the pastures, she was quiet and timid. Later I found out that she had heard about my position in Nebuchadnezzar's court; she had been intimidated in that first encounter. Having been enchanted by my first vision of her, I sought to engage Rachel in conversation to discern more about her character, but all I got for my efforts were monosyllabic grunts, which I was left to interpret as I chose. However, her beauty provided me with sufficient motivation to keep attempting to engage her in conversation and penetrate her reserve. When I spoke about Abba and Isaac during their childhood, she faced me briefly and unleashed her radiant smile upon me as she recalled some of those interactions. Because I had been unprepared for such dazzling beauty, her effulgence stunned me, causing me to stumble over my words. Ironically, when she perceived my discomfort, she regained her own bearings.

As soon as she felt less intimidated, Rachel unleashed a torrent of pent-up words that surprised me. Though she began at the same topic—the relationship between our fathers—her flow soon morphed into a description of how horrible things had been in Jerusalem in the months and years before they had left. "All the horrors that prophet Jeremiah forecast had come true. Starvation and pestilence overran the streets; people were dying all around us..." It was clear that she was, by nature, both observant of the events around her and descriptive in her speech. Later, I realized that I had probably received a better idea of the conditions in my old home city from Rachel than I had from any other source. But it was not only her words and observations. As she felt free to talk, she became animated, and she gestured freely and gracefully. For that space of time, she seemed uninhibited; we interacted as old friends, yet there was also the tinge of romance there. During that period of free gesticulation and expression, she completed the task of capturing my heart.

To prolong our interactions, I gave to her a virtually unabridged view of my lands, showing her various areas of good pastureland and pointing out the wells in the areas where streams were uncertain. Their flock was small compared to mine, so I invited her to mix her sheep and goats with mine. I could easily afford for my relatives to mistakenly claim a few of mine as their own.

As we walked back to the house, I mentioned an employment opportunity to her. "I have recently had an unexpected opening. A fortnight ago, my shepherd, who has been with me for the last four years, announced his intention of joining the military. He will be leaving next week. Though I had planned to look for a replacement among the Chaldean youths, perhaps that plan isn't the best one." She looked at me hopefully, so I proceeded. To keep up an unimpeded flow of words, I kept my eyes directed away from her overpoweringly lovely visage. I wanted to forestall the return of my vocal stumbling.

"The times of transition are difficult for all families. If you took this job, it would mean a steady flow of money for your father. I think he would feel more comfortable accepting contributions from you than he would from me. Your salary would make him feel less dependent. It's not that I'd begrudge giving him any money, for I love Isaac as did Abba, but I know he'll do better if he can feel independent and settled as soon as possible. That sense of succeeding will make his transition to Babylon much easier for him. Moreover, I'll encourage your family to stay with me for several months, so the work will be convenient for you. You can care for your father's stock as you watch over mine. I'll hire a young Chaldean boy to be with you. He can be your assistant, run errands for you, and teach you the language." During most of my soliloquy, I was looking at the grass or over at the horizon. Her dazzling eyes had unnerved me earlier. I worried that I would start tripping over my words again if I permitted myself the pleasure of gazing into her eyes. But when I completed my soliloquy, I looked to see how she had received my words.

She had been silent during the entire harangue, so I was surprised when I looked over and saw a tear rolling down her cheek. Alarmed, I queried, "Rachel, why are you crying? Have I said something to upset you? The last thing in the world I wanted to do was to offend you or your family's pride."

"Have no fear. Your words have been gentle, welcoming, and far from offensive. On the contrary," she said, trying to smile as she wiped away her tears, "your words are just what I've been longing to hear and what our family has needed. This period of transition has traumatized us all, particularly Abba. After Mama died last year, he made the decision for us to leave Judea and come here. He believed the words of the prophet Jeremiah, but since making the decision to come to Babylon, everything has seemed so difficult, uncertain, verging on disastrous. During the last few weeks in Jerusalem, the suffering was far worse than anything that we had previously experienced. There was almost no food, the death tolls mount far more rapidly, and the king's forces were harshly enforcing the ban on desertion."

"We had to sneak out of Jerusalem the night after Abba left. He deceived the guards to obtain leave to exit the city. He told them that he was going to check on his vineyard, which was located south of Jerusalem, because he hadn't heard any news from there for several months, which actually was true. When he checked on our flock, he was dismayed to find that our sheep and goats had been scattered and decimated by the surrounding troops. The few remaining animals came to him as their shepherd, but several of them died on the way. The Chaldean soldiers were actually decent to us during our foray, but leaving the place of our birth and knowing we'd never see Jerusalem again have inflicted their own emotional traumas. Therefore, I've been praying that God would send us a sign that we hadn't made a mistake sneaking out of Jerusalem and coming to Babylon. After hearing your words of encouragement, I think you just may be that sign."

"Well, I'm pleased," I said, trying in vain to hide just how pleased I was. "The transition period is always hard, but I believe you'll do well here. If Isaac has a heart like Abba—and I believe he does—he'll adjust. Over time, he'll come to see the hand of God in bringing him here."

"I see it already." Rachel beamed, reached out, and took my hand. "I'll help Abba come to see Adonai's hand in everything." Taking my hand was meant to be a simple gesture of friendship, but by the time we had returned to the house, she had taken complete possession of my heart. I was enchanted to the core.

Their transition went smoothly and more so than for most families because of our relationship. Just having a familiar face here, particularly someone who was fairly high up in the court of Nebuchadnezzar, greatly eased their anxieties. Isaac was happy to renew his relationship with my mother because they had always enjoyed each other's company. Within a few weeks, she became his chief emotional support and confidant.

Like everyone else, Isaac, his sons-in-law, and two sons received land. Their combined allotment amounted to a good-sized parcel of land about a league out of Babylon. They worked the land, planted their seeds, and soon had a decent yield. With Rachel bringing in money and the flocks regaining their health in the good pastures, the family navigated the transition well. Soon they turned their minds to sending down deeper roots, with the goal of making Babylon their new home, just as God through Jeremiah had instructed them to do.

Isaac had been able to obtain some gold before things in Jerusalem became desperate. He held on to it despite the shortages, knowing how important it would be when they got to Babylon. About six weeks after their arrival, Isaac informed me of his desire to become a shopkeeper. His gold gave him sufficient capital so that he could make the necessary purchases and a start in the business. My friend Hananiah was more involved in facilitating the immigrants' entry into business such as trade, so I introduced them. My sister Elizabeth also had secured a modicum of gold, but it was not enough to consider going into business alone. However, she was interested in partnering with Isaac, so she went with Isaac when I made the introduction.

Hananiah was able to steer Isaac toward some traders who had a reputation for being honest. He also directed Isaac to a section of the city where shops were not overly abundant and the exiles were beginning to find their feet. In such a location, the chances for success were high. The exiles would make good customers when the shop was established. From my experience of counseling those in transition, I was able to advise him about some items that all families needed, both as they arrived and when they became more settled, so he was able to establish a store that carried many of the needed items. Isaac and Elizabeth were careful with their money. Soon their store showed signs of becoming one of the more prosperous establishments among the exiles in Babylon.

As I saw Isaac making the necessary steps to engraft his family into Babylon, I approached him about Rachel. "Isaac, I have a strong desire to know Rachel better. Though I tried to elude deportation to Babylon, my years here have caused me to grow in my faith and confidence in the goodness and wisdom of the Lord. In the letter from Jeremiah that I read to the exiles, the Lord commands us to settle in this land, marry, and raise families. I believe that I'm in a position to obey that injunction at this point in my life. From the interactions I have had with Rachel since your arrival, I believe that she may be the woman I'd like to pursue with the goal of marriage, but I will cease immediately if you refuse to give me your blessing on the endeavor." Some virtuous men have declared that it is unfair for a man to court a woman when she feels anxious and unstable. Let them rejoice in their own self-imposed righteousness. I felt no compulsion to abide by their codes. I experienced no remorse in seeking to woo Rachel.

"You have both my blessing and my good will," replied Isaac. "My daughter is a fine woman. I'm convinced she'll make someone a great wife. You remind me greatly of your father, a man whom I've admired all my life, and that gives me a favorable impression of you as a husband for Rachel. In addition, I'm obliged to you for the timely help that you gave to our family during this transition. Therefore, I'm pleased that you want to marry my daughter. Shall I speak with her?"

"With your permission, I'll take the next step, even if that violates our cultural traditions. Because I've received you into my home, Rachel might feel compelled to give a favorable answer, even if her heart is against it. I need to be sure that she doesn't respond out of a sense of obligation. In our initial interactions, she gave me indications that she enjoyed my company, but I want to assess her heart more thoroughly. I need to be sure that I can I turn her friendship into more amorous feelings before putting the question to her. If I sense that she's able to respond to me with heartfelt emotions, I'll tell her of your consent and blessing for our union."

Isaac's approval left me in too much of a flutter to attend to anything else, so I set aside my plans for the day. I was determined to find out where I stool with Rachel. My sudden appearance in the pastures startled her. Though we had not interacted privately since the day of their arrival, the changes in her countenance and posture at my approach led me to think she did not regard my surprise visitation as unpleasant. After greeting her, I walked with her through the fields, attempting to hide the purpose of my visit while I worked up my nerve. I pointed out some of the better land for pasturing, which was somewhat redundant from our previous encounter. Though she seemed a bit more relaxed as our conversation proceeded, I also detected a degree of deflation in her posture and countenance as I regurgitated the same information from our previous encounter, so I stopped.

"Rachel, I didn't come here to show you pastures. It's time for me be honest. The reason I came out had nothing to do with shepherding. I came out to spend time with you. I feel compelled to get to know you better. The shepherding issues were only a screen to hide my true motive. The first time we met, you captivated my heart. From that first encounter, I decided that I had to get to know you more deeply. I had to find out if you really were the woman I thought you were. I waited until Isaac was settled before approaching him about you. You have such a lovely face and a wise countenance, and you move more gracefully than any woman I've ever seen. In our family's conversations, I sensed that you have strong faith, a bright mind, and quick comprehension. In short, you seem to epitomize the qualities that would make a great wife. You're everything I've been looking for in the woman I hope to marry."

"Though perhaps it isn't gallant of me to attempt to woo you until you're settled, I don't really care. Maybe by courting you before others are aware of your beauty and character, I may have a chance to win your heart." My heart was pounding and my words came out a bit shrill as I completed my soliloquy. Never before had I spoken to a woman in that manner. Indeed, since I was abducted at such an early age, I had rarely spoken to any women at all, except in my official capacity. Without question, my words were far too forward and frank, but I was speaking the words of my heart.

At first, it seemed to me that she was offended. She walked on in silence for a few minutes, which caused me to be afraid that my boldness had insulted her or frightened her into muteness. When I tried to obtain a glimpse of her face, she took steps to make that impossible. After a bit, however, she turned to face me and looked deeply into my eyes. "Your declaration took me by surprise, so I needed some time to consider what you just told me and how I should respond, but I'm pleased with what you've said. There's no reason for you to be gallant and wait for me to become more settled. I'm pleased that you desire to woo me."

"Do you think no word of Babylon ever made it to Jerusalem? We've all heard how you, Hananiah, and Mishael defied the king. We were all amazed to hear how Adonai spared your lives in the king's furnace. What an adventure! What a man of faith you've become! When I knew I was coming here, I hoped to get to know you. Now you're telling me that you want to court and marry me. That's better than a dream. So let me be equally frank. I have no desire for you to wait until I'm settled. You're in a good position to win my affections if you pursue me, so keep trying. Indeed, I think you might have won my heart the first day I was here," she replied, with a slightly choked voice as she again took my hand.

With such encouragement from both Isaac and Rachel, it was unlikely that I would fail. I encouraged her father to remain with my family long after their needs of transition had been met. We had many evenings together, usually with several members of the family. As I got to know her better, my interest and affection for Rachel grew steadily, for I found that the promise of her eyes was true. She had true depth of character and intelligence. Had we been in Jerusalem, Jewish society would have forced us to wait two years, but that custom, like so many others, was disrupted in our exile. Eight months after their arrival, Rachel and I were wed.

CHAPTER EIGHT

Changes within the Group

RACHEL AND I WERE NOT THE ONLY LOVERS IN OUR GROUP. Ours was not the only wedding that occurred during that year. When Elizabeth went with Isaac to meet Hananiah, she had wanted to establish a partnership with our cousin to open a store; their combined funds would improve their financial stability. They decided that day to pool their resources, which provided a strong economic foundation for their enterprise. However, the most important partnership that sprung from that day involved Hananiah. He met several times with Elizabeth and Isaac to discuss issues regarding the store, but after three weeks, he gave up the facade of disinterestedness. He came to my mother, Ruth, and me to get permission to court Elizabeth. For several months, as I was courting Rachel, Hananiah was courting Elizabeth. Instead of squelching our intimacy, the addition of another couple during that time multiplied our enjoyment. Three months after Rachel and I became one flesh, Hananiah and Elizabeth were wed.

My sister took up the role of Rachel's mentor during the transition. Rachel's mother was dead, but Elizabeth had been through the process of courting and preparing for marriage. Moreover, although I had been away from my family for years, Elizabeth knew me as well as anyone did. She could tell Rachel about my strengths and warn her about my limitations and quirks. Perhaps my sister lessened the luster that Rachel may have felt in anticipating our union, but it was probably advantageous for my bride to have a more realistic view of me prior to the wedding. During those months, Elizabeth and Rachel grew more intimate; they have remained close friends and confidants during the subsequent years.

What could I attempt to say about wedded life that is not hackneyed or trite? Rachel proved to be the woman that I had anticipated and more. The same could be said of Elizabeth with Hananiah. Our married life was not pure bliss. I do not believe that complete rapture ever occurs in marriage. Do any of us think that God really intended our lives for unalloyed pleasure? Rachel and I have had our struggles, but we have had plenty of joys and pleasures to counterbalance the pain that invariably accompanies the union of two people. Rachel became a great wife and mother, exceeding all my expectations for her in both areas—or at least the realistic ones.

To a large degree, our quartet was already incorporated into Chaldean society through our positions in Nebuchadnezzar's court, but I led the way to a deeper immersion into the Babylonian culture by marrying Rachel. Though I was the first out of the quartet to wed, Hananiah and Elizabeth quickly followed. Within a year, Mishael also secured a bride from among the Jewish refugees.

I was privileged to play a role in that relationship as well. Years earlier, Abba had known Samuel, a priest who immigrated to Babylon with his family about a year after Isaac and his family had come. Naomi was his oldest daughter. Within days of my introductory speech, Samuel came to me hoping to rekindle the relationship that we had had through Abba. He hoped that I could help him obtain employment as a clerk. My colleague Mishael had more administrative responsibility in that area. When I took Samuel to meet Mishael, Naomi accompanied us. As it had been with Elizabeth and Hananiah, during the time Mishael was ostensibly helping Samuel find a clerical position, his eye was on Naomi. Using previously successful tactics that had been employed by Hananiah, Mishael met with the two of them several times to discuss Samuel's skills and qualifications so that he could find the best position for him. But within a month, the pretense was dropped. After getting Samuel set up as a clerk, Mishael sought to establish his position with

Naomi. This time, Rachel took upon herself the role of mentor for the new bride-to-be. Because of that relationship, she and Rachel became close friends, and they remained close over the years. Elizabeth also took Naomi under her wings. Over the years, the brides became as close as the three of us.

Daniel, the brightest, handsomest, and most faithful of our group—the one who would have probably been the best husband—was the only member of the quartet to remain single. Many families entertained him in hopes of engaging his interest in one of their daughters. Though Daniel invariably appeared to enjoy their company, he never showed any particular interest in the women that he met. He never commented on his plans, but it seemed to me that he felt his responsibilities excluded matrimony.

Several years passed with their usual mixture of trials and blessings. Though you might expect that being in Babylon inured us to the troubles in Jerusalem, to ignore the debacles of our home would have been a denial of our heritage and Jewishness. We were the physical descendants of Abraham. We were deeply concerned about the tragic unfolding of events in the land of our births. Moreover, we all still had members of our extended families in Jerusalem. Although all of my immediate family had left Jerusalem and made it to Babylon before the total destruction of our greatest city took place, Daniel and Hananiah still had members of their immediate families in Jerusalem when the walls were breached. They were anxious to gather any available information. Mishael was like me. The members of his immediate family were already in Babylon, but he was concerned about his extended family members who were still there. We all took advantage of every opportunity to hear about the situation in Jerusalem and our families, although all the information that we received was discouraging.

We had settled in Babylon, and we were fulfilling the exhortation of God through Jeremiah to establish families and incorporate ourselves into the community. Since our abduction, we had become accustomed to the reality that virtually all the news that we received about Jerusalem was disheartening. However, a substantial escalation of unfavorable news had occurred during the period when the three of us had met our wives and started our families.

Still, all of us were shocked and dismayed when word of the complete destruction of Jerusalem's wall and temple made its way to Babylon. The four of us had been taken captive when King Jehoiakim had proved himself a fool and refused to pay the tribute that had been due to Nebuchadnezzar and his realm. Almost unbelievably, the same thing had occurred with his brother King Zedekiah about a decade later. Instead of listening to Jeremiah, the true prophet, the monarch encircled himself with false prophets, who repeated the same drivel that had undermined his brother's reign. King Zedekiah was persuaded by the false prophet's flattery and deceptive encouragement, so he withheld the tribute that was due to King Nebuchadnezzar. He was a victim to the Chaldeans in a manner that was eerily similar to the disaster that had engulfed his brother.

However this time, Nebuchadnezzar was in no mood for gentleness. The Chaldean monarch made King Zedekiah and Jerusalem suffer for his rebellion. The temple was razed, the city walls were torn down, and the gates were burned. It was the king's final judgment on our land. The destruction fulfilled the dismal prophecies that Jeremiah had warned our people would occur. The king was brought to Babylon as a blind captive. He was fettered in bronze, and his eye sockets drained hideously after the punishment he had received. We heard that his wives were violated, and his sons were killed in front of him immediately prior to his eyes being burned out. I believed the rumors. Nebuchadnezzar was not a king who tolerated rebellion in any of his conquered lands. This was the second incident of rebellion from Jerusalem. He wanted the Jews and all other conquered lands to understand how seriously he would treat their acts of rebellion.

News of the destruction of Jerusalem's wall and temple took its toll upon us. Though we were obeying God's exhortation to transfer our loyalty to Babylon, we were still disheartened when we heard about the destruction of our homeland and birthplace. None of us harbored any secret hope of returning to Jerusalem, but we all had emotional ties to the Jewish capital. My father had been buried there, as were the majority of my relatives and Abba's antecedents. The same was true for my colleagues. The desecration of our forefathers' resting places sent shafts of pain and regret into each of our hearts.

By the time the news of Jerusalem's destruction reached us, Rachel and I had a child with a second on the way. Despite her pregnancy, Rachel continued to take an active role in assisting the settling of the new arrivals during that dramatic period. Many of them were among the most traumatized that we had ever seen. The numbers of exiles were fewer than we had expected because so many had died during the siege and subsequent overthrow of Jerusalem. Most of the survivors were weak. Many were diseased. A high percentage of the men had suffered wounds in their futile attempt to defend Jerusalem. Many of those wounds festered and eventually proved mortal. Many of the wounded had died along the way. A substantial number survived until reaching Babylon but died shortly afterward. Though we had transferred our loyalty to Babylon, knowledge of the destruction of our home and the visible reminder of those survivors repeatedly stabbed our hearts.

CHAPTER NINE

The Second Great Dream

D ANIEL WAS A FREQUENT GUEST AT OUR HOME DURING
those years. He seemed comfortable around Rachel and
enjoyed playing uncle to our children, so we always sought his
company when he was Babylon. We were flattered that he seemed to
enjoy coming to our home because he had demands on his time from so
many directions. It was no exaggeration to say that he had become the
second most important figure in Babylon. He was immediately under
the king.

Nebuchadnezzar had intentionally placed our leader in that position
shortly after Daniel had interpreted the king's mysterious dream, but
the hearts of the people had not been convinced. By the time of my
marriage, Daniel was ubiquitously recognized as second-in-command.
He had demonstrated his value to the realm over and again. Even his
enemies had to acknowledge Daniel's value to the realm. Whenever
there were significant administrative needs in distant areas of the realm
that the king could not address personally, he sent Daniel. Because the
realm was extensive and the conquered nations numerous, that position
of trust required Daniel to leave Babylon frequently, typically for long
stretches of time.

One evening when he had just returned from a prolonged visit to
Ecbatana, he joined us for a meal. I surprised him with some recent news

from Babylon. "Have you heard about the king's most recent dream?" I asked.

"No, I haven't heard anything. As you know, I've been in Ecbatana and attending to a number of issues in that section of the kingdom and just returned today. My arrival was fairly late, so I haven't had a chance to update the king or receive any messages from him. Tell me what you've heard," replied my friend, who was somewhat surprised by and genuinely curious about my announcement.

"Though I've heard nothing directly from the king, several of my subordinates told me that the king is really distressed about another dream that he recently had. From everything I can gather, Nebuchadnezzar seems to placed extreme importance on this dream. This time, he can remember the dream, but he is even more upset than he was with the previous dream. Again, he is convinced that this is a message from the gods. He was anxious enough that he tried to get help from some of the Chaldeans in his court, but none of his sages and counselors could interpret the dream's meaning. Their inability to give him an interpretation has made him more edgy. I think you'd better be ready for him to call you into his chambers in the next day or so."

Daniel looked thoughtful. He mumbled quietly, "Thank you for the warning. Though I've heard nothing about this, by what you tell me of the king's reaction, I'm sure this will prove important. The king doesn't panic easily. I'll let you know what happens."

In fact, the king called Daniel the next day, without the pretense of other motives. After a brief greeting and a couple of questions about Ecbatana, the king related the contents of the dream to my friend.

Daniel came back to us three days later and related the whole incident. "I have no doubt that before I went to him, the king knew that the dream bore ominous warnings. Though my interpretation for him was not what he wanted to hear, I believe he felt some comfort in being able to relate the dream to me and hear what I had to say. Uncertainty has to be more distressing than knowing the worst, although my interpretation was far from favorable." Of course, Rachel and I were attentive to Daniel's words.

"The king said to me, 'As I was lying on my bed, there came to my mind a vision of a great tree. The tree was wondrous. It was not only taller than all the other trees but also had abundant limbs that extended twenty to thirty cubits in all directions and covered a vast area of the countryside. The great tree was visible in all directions. It appeared majestic to the eyes of all who beheld it. In the branches of the tree, numerous birds were making their nests. The expanse of limbs created a shelter that was the home of various kinds of animals. Moreover, the tree was fruitful and bore an abundant crop that all the animals fed upon. In short, the tree was by far the greatest in all the land.'"

"'As I contemplated the majesty and beneficial nature of the tree, I heard an angelic voice cry out, "Chop down the great tree, lop off the branches, chase away the birds and animals, and scatter the foliage and fruit." The command was obeyed immediately, leaving only a stump and roots behind. Then the angel called out again, "Let a band of iron and bronze be placed around the stump of the tree. Let it stand in the grasses of the field and be drenched with dew. Let his mind be changed from that of a man to that of a beast and let him feed upon the grasses like the cattle. Let seven periods of time pass over him until such a time when he'll come to understand that there is only one sovereign in all of creation: the Most High God who rules over all humankind. He must be instructed, and he must come to realize that Adonai bestows power and greatness on those whom he chooses, but he humbles the proud who exalt themselves."' That was the essence of the dream that the king related to me," said Daniel. The countenance of my friend bore witness to his distress on the king's account.

"No wonder the king was anxious. The whole dream sounds ominous," I said. "What did you say to the king?"

"For several minutes, I was too dismayed to speak. Finally, the king said, 'Belteshazzar, don't be distressed on my account. I need to hear the interpretation, even if its unfavorable.' I replied, 'Oh, my king, if only the dream applied to those who hate you and the interpretation to your enemies rather than to yourself. As I think you have already concluded, the great tree represents you. Who else could be described in such glorious terms such as reaching to the heavens and supplying fruit and shelter for all around? You're the mighty king, and your majesty has been witnessed by all. Regrettably, the angelic proclamation to chop down the tree, cut off its branches, and place a band of iron and bronze around the stump also applies to you. But there was also good news in the vision. He commanded them to leave the stump and roots in the new grass of the field until seven periods have passed over him.

"'The angelic being foretold bad times that lie ahead for you. Yet the angelic proclamation did not leave us without hope. You'll be struck down and driven from humankind. You'll become wild like the beasts of the field. You'll be chained, eat the grass around you like cattle, and drenched with the dew from heaven until seven years have passed. After the sentence upon you has been served, your mind will be restored. You'll come to recognize that Adonai is the One True God, the Lord Almighty. When your mind is restored, God will also restore your kingdom to you.' I spoke frankly to the king because there was no way to soften the blow."

"As you can imagine, the king and I were downcast and quiet. Finally, the king aroused himself and asked, 'What do you recommend?' I said, 'My advice to you, Oh, king, is to humble yourself before the Lord. Beginning today, recognize that Adonai is the only God in heaven. Worship the One True God and him alone. Be righteous in your reign, just to your subjects, generous to the poor. Adonai is gracious. If you truly humble yourself before the Lord, the great dream may prove to be a warning rather than a definite forecast. Perhaps the horrible vision may be averted.' There was nothing else I could think to tell him." Daniel's mien was melancholy, and his eyes were downcast.

CHAPTER TEN

Protecting the King's Interests

A FTER DANIEL RELATED HIS INTERPRETATION OF THE dream and his recommendations, I asked, "What's your real opinion of the dream? Do you think the declaration of the angel is final? Is the calamity inevitably to come upon the king, or do you think there is real hope that Nebuchadnezzar might avoid the angel's sentence?"

"In truth, there was nothing in the dream to make me think that the horrors might be avoided, but we know that Adonai is gracious. The advice I gave him was sound. I believe that if the king truly humbles himself and sincerely worships the One True God, the Lord may show mercy to our king, but I must admit that I'm not optimistic. Though we can hope that the vision may serve more as a warning than a sentence, I see nothing about Nebuchadnezzar to encourage me that he could ever have such a complete change of heart on his own, as much as I love and admire the king," replied Daniel. His countenance reflected his oppressed spirits.

I reached over and gripped his arm. "My friend, it is clear that you really love the king. So do I. Though he is a pagan and a despot who has threatened our lives unjustly in the past, in truth, he has been better to us than most conquerors would have been to their subjects in captivity. Even though I think your advice to him was appropriate, I share your pessimism. How likely is it that Nebuchadnezzar will humble himself sufficiently to avoid the fulfillment of the angelic proclamation? However, it does the king no good for us to be bogged down and oppressed in gloom. We must think of a way to preserve his throne and protect his interests during his seven years of humiliation, if the events transpire as the dream foretold."

Daniel remained silent for some time and then replied, "You're right. Becoming depressed over possibilities that we can't alter won't help Nebuchadnezzar or the realm. If we are to honor Adonai during this time, the critical step is for us to do what we can to facilitate the king's return to the throne when this nightmare is finished, if, in fact, the dream unfolds as it has been forecast. What do you suggest that we should do?"

"I think that the critical issue is who has the authority if the king is taken out of commission in the manner that the dream suggests. You're the man that the king trusts more than any other in the kingdom and rightly so. You are his wisest counselor, and you've also proven your trustworthiness to him many times. The king knows that you have no desire to usurp his position. He understands how safe his realm would be in your hands and how readily you would take steps to restore him to the throne at the completion of the sentence. My suggestion is that we have the king put a system in place to transfer his authority to you, in case this dream is fulfilled and he becomes unfit to rule. From the description the king gave of his dream, it appears to me that the angel's pronouncement and the subsequent disasters will come about suddenly and unexpectedly. In consequence, the king will be in no position to do anything at that time."

"Though I agree with you in general, to succeed, we must come up with a plan that includes and satisfies Prince Belshazzar," replied my friend, "and the plan must be realistic. The crown prince will not sit back and allow me to assume all the power of his father, irrespective of any provisions by Nebuchadnezzar. We have to come up with a plan that appeases Prince Belshazzar, but one that keeps the absolute authority out of his hands."

"You're absolutely right; I think Belshazzar could be the greatest impediment to his father's regaining the throne. If he were to rule in his father's stead for seven years, it would take a civil war to restore Nebuchadnezzar to the throne when the sentence is completed. The best thing would be to facilitate a means by which the true authority of the throne can be transferred to you with the appearance of some combination of power. Perhaps the best scenario would be that the crown prince sits upon the throne in the king's absence, but every important decision that arises needs to be made by you or perhaps a triumvirate of the prince, the queen, and you." I stopped for a moment to ponder and then said, "That would work. With the king's blessing, we set up the triumvirate to receive the king's authority, should the need arise and he cannot fulfill his obligations. At the same time, we get Nebuchadnezzar to make sure that the queen sides with you in every important decision. Though I don't really know the prince, it's easy to imagine that if he tastes the full power of the throne while the king is deposed, he may be hard to displace when it's time for his father to be restored. We must do all in our power to prevent a full-blown civil war when it's time to restore Nebuchadnezzar to the throne."

"Moreover, Belshazzar wouldn't be the first prince to hasten the demise of his father because of his lust for power, particularly if he found the king in the extremely vulnerable position that the dream suggests. If the king makes it official that the prince can only experience a portion of the power rather than the absolute sovereignty of the throne, he won't be as great of an obstacle to overcome when the time of restoration comes. Of course, the other issue is what to do with the king himself. If this sentence falls upon the king, I think he should be sequestered in a place where he's hidden from public view. That place should remain secret from everyone except those who have to know. In particular, Prince Belshazzar should be kept ignorant of the location of the king's sequestration."

"You say that you don't know Prince Belshazzar, but you make recommendations as if you do. Many a prince might be willing to commit regicide if he had a convenient way to kill his father and a clear path to the throne. However, if I was forced to name one prince whom I would most suspect to be capable of carrying out such an atrocity against his own father, it would be Belshazzar. Without question, this situation will make Nebuchadnezzar vulnerable," replied Daniel, clearly deep in thought. "The more I contemplate your recommendations, the more I agree with you. The best thing we can do for the king is to keep the prince's hands from becoming too attached to the scepter. The four of us should approach the king and present your ideas. Indeed, we should do it quickly. We need to get the steps for the transfer of authority in place as soon as possible, for if this dream is fulfilled, it will probably occur quickly and without warning."

Three days later, our quartet appeared before the king. Nebuchadnezzar was still somewhat subdued because his thoughts dwelt on the dream and Daniel's interpretation, but he welcomed us warmly, declaring, "It has been many months since I have had the pleasure of hosting the four of you together. Though I'm always glad to see some of the wisest and most loyal men in my realm, I cannot help but think this unwonted visit is for more than just the exchange of pleasantries." He paused, smiled, and then continued, "I strongly suspect that the four of you coming to me relates in some manner to my disturbing dream."

Hananiah had been appointed spokesman since the plan involved the king consigning his trust and authority to Daniel and the plan had originated with me. He declared, "Oh, king, may your reign be long and prosperous. You're too wise for us to come before you without you discerning the motive behind our visit even before we speak. As you've deduced, the four of us have discussed your situation and have some recommendations that we think you should strongly consider.

"First of all, be assured that we have discussed this issue in utter confidentiality. None of us has even talked with our wives, although we may get Abed-nego to change that, depending on your response to our suggestions. Second, we all think Belteshazzar's advice to you was appropriate. We all heartily endorse it. Humble yourself, worship Adonai, and reign justly over your subjects, particularly the vulnerable members of our society. The God of Israel is merciful. He may relent of his plans to bring this calamity upon your majesty if you truly humble yourself before him. More than a century ago, the prophet Jonah was sent to Nineveh to pronounce condemnation upon that city, but the king and all the people humbled themselves; the disaster was averted. We hope the same will be true for you. Third, we think it's wise to make contingency plans in case your majesty is deposed for a time. The details of the dream lead us to believe that if the sentence takes place, it will come suddenly and without warning. Though we don't want to cast any aspersions upon your son, we could foresee some difficulty in your return to the throne if, while you were deposed, Prince Belshazzar obtains the absolute power and sovereignty that you now possess." Hananiah stopped to allow the king to consider his words.

King Nebuchadnezzar chuckled to himself and said, "I'm in total agreement with that assessment. Though I'm not sure how many princes could be trusted in that situation, I'm convinced that Belshazzar isn't one of them."

Hananiah smiled. "Because of that reality, we have composed a document outlining the steps to be taken should you become temporarily incapable of holding office. In the document, we state that should Your Highness be deposed for a time, the power of the throne would be shared between your queen, your son, and Belteshazzar, your most trusted adviser. Though Prince Belshazzar will wear your robe and sit on the throne, each of the triumvirate would have equal authority in all questions of state. We suggest that the document be witnessed by the principal magistrates of the land, with your authority bequeathed to them to put in motion the plans that have been outlined, should the need arise. The queen should be the one to notify the magistrates of the need to implement the plan. There is also a provision to remove any member of the triumvirate who seeks to override or depose one of the other members. This will make it clear to Belshazzar that any attempt to usurp the triumvirate or overpower his mother will cause him to lose his position and all his power. All questions of policy and procedure must be agreed upon by two thirds of the triumvirate. Though we did not state this in the memorandum, we think you should discuss with the queen the importance of her siding with Daniel in all disputes and questions of policy." Nebuchadnezzar nodded in agreement with that plan.

"The other important consideration, which we have included in a separate memorandum, is that if you should be incapacitated for a time, especially in the manner suggested by the dream, you will be taken to a place away from general observation. The dream suggests that you would be wild and would have to be restrained. It isn't a picture we want widely dispersed. We're sure that you feel the same way. The whereabouts of your person should be kept in strict confidentially. Only the queen and a few select others should know your location. Your son would not be one of the number. Of course, such measures would only be taken if they become necessary. If necessity dictates, we would want your majesty to be hidden from the view of all of your subjects, except for those who have to care for you. We don't want your son to know where you are so that he isn't tempted to try something deplorable."

The king smiled wanly at Hananiah's phraseology. "I'm determined to follow Belteshazzar's advice. I hope none of this will be necessary, but I agree with your caution in coming up with a contingency plan. I think the steps that you've outlined are wise, and they will facilitate the happy ending that the dream promises if the sad intermediary steps come into play. For three days, let me review the proposal regarding the sharing of power. If I still find the proposal proper, we'll make it an official proclamation before the twenty leading magistrates of the land. As for the second document, it's wise for it to be witnessed only by the six of us: the four of you, my wife, and me. If I become like the image from the dream, I don't want others to gawk at my humiliation, particularly my son. I want my location to be known by as few people as possible."

Three days later, the king met with us again. Over that interval, he had related to the queen the dream, the interpretation by Daniel, and the recommendations from us, including her vital role in the entire process. He completely agreed to our plan as we had outlined it. He had made it clear to the queen how critical it was that she side with Daniel in all questions of state. She needed to trust that Daniel knew the king's wishes and would take steps to protect his interests. He stressed how vital it was for her to withstand any appeals from their son. Within a week, he signed the manuscript before twenty leading Chaldean magistrates, making the document the law of the land until the time that it was repealed by him—the king. The signing was witnessed by the queen, the crown prince, and Daniel—the principal players.

The three of us stayed away from the signing, hoping to reduce the likelihood of connecting us to the proposal, although I am sure some did. Several of the magistrates had heard something about a disturbing dream the king had experienced. Perhaps they wondered if these measures had anything to do with his mysterious nocturnal visitation, but besides the king and the three of us, Daniel had made the interpretation known to no one. Each of us had held our tongues. The crown prince did not act suspicious as to why such contingencies were being addressed. He seemed satisfied that he would hold the scepter and sit on the throne as the acting king, with at least a share of the power in the event of his father's indisposition. I also suspect that he thought he could woo his mother to his side in the majority of the state's decisions.

As to the second matter, we agreed that the king would be sheltered at my demesne. My home was farther from the center of Babylon than that of the rest of quartet. The land around my home was more extensive because we kept numerous livestock, and I owned my own grazing land. Because the king would be harbored at my demesne, Nebuchadnezzar was introduced to my wife Rachel.

When she was presented to the king, she said, "Your Highness, though I know that I have been brought here for a different reason, I've wanted to say something to you since my arrival. I cannot let this opportunity pass without thanking you for the kind reception that you organized for the exiles. Like so many others, my family was truly shaken by the experience of fleeing Jerusalem, but the steps you took to make our reception kind and welcoming made it so much easier for us. Though I realize that my husband made it especially easy for my family because we were related, I've spoken with many other families. To a man, they express their appreciation for the kindness and the welcome that you showed our people during that difficult time. We all have praised Adonai for giving us a kind and wise leader." She paused and looked empathetically at the king and resumed, saying, "Azariah told me of the reason for this visit. Though the possibilities that lie ahead of you frighten me, and I join my husband and his colleagues in hoping we never need to take these steps, I assure you that if they become necessary, I will personally attend Your Highness and make sure that you're treated well."

Though he was the king, she was moved by a desire to comfort someone she felt was in distress. She laid her hand on the king's arm as a gesture of kindness and goodwill. I was sure that she acted without thinking. Though she would not presume to take liberties with the king, I was afraid the king would take the gesture amiss. Instead, he patted her hand and replied, "Thank you, my dear. Though I hope none of this comes to pass, I am reassured by meeting you. I believe that if the unthinkable occurs, I'd rather be under your care than anyone I know."

For a year, all seemed to go well. There were no overt challenges to the authority of the realm. The quartet went about our normal work. Nothing untoward happened with respect to the fulfillment of the dream. The king met regularly with Daniel and some of the Jewish priests who were in exile. Every week he met with Samuel, Mishael's father-in-law, and the priest taught him about Abraham and the special relationship between his descendants and Adonai. In many ways, the king did seem humbled and had a genuine desire to appease Adonai. About the time that I began to hope that our assessment of the king's ability to change had been too pessimistic, Daniel came to our home in the middle of the night. He seemed distressed. "A messenger came to me from the queen. She was quite upset and said that I needed to come to the palace right away. I want you to go with me because I suspect this has to do with the fulfillment of the dream."

When we arrived, the queen was hysterical. She was weeping, trembling, and wringing her hands. She looked so pitiable that I began to think that we were called for her sake, but as she calmed down, she related, "The king and I were walking over this rooftop enjoying a lovely evening as we looked over our beautiful city. We had just had a wonderful meal, and the king felt quite expansive. He has this way of puffing out his chest and throwing his head back when he feels particularly well. As I leaned upon his shoulder, he pointed out many of the wonders of Babylon, particularly the hanging gardens and some of the most prominent buildings. He went into detail about the amazing architecture of the city. He pointed out some of the unique features of the more remarkable buildings."

"As his eyes scanned the rooftops of Babylon, he took a large breath and boasted, 'Just think about this, my dear. This city, indeed the entire realm, are here because of my great wisdom and power.' As soon as the words were out of his mouth, there came a loud, deep rumble, which seemed like thunder, yet it almost sounded like words. As I have thought about it, I really think it was the voice of God or an angel. Suddenly King Nebuchadnezzar fell unconscious at my feet. When he woke, he was snarling and acting like a wild animal. The only response that I could get from him sounded like a growl or a hiss." She closed her eyes for a moment and gave an involuntary shudder. After a couple of moments, she recovered and asked through her tears, "Do you think this is the fulfillment of his dream?"

Daniel replied, "Though we cannot be certain until we've observed him for some days, I believe it is. You did well to send for us and no one else. It's critically important that you tell no one else what has happened. Do you trust the servant that you sent to me?"

"I do," she replied while regaining her composure. "He has been with the king for years, and he has demonstrated his loyalty and trustworthiness over and again. I'm sure he will betray nothing; I trust him more than anyone I know."

"Good. You've done well. We'll need his help, but let's involve no one else. The best thing to do right away is to move the king to the home of Abed-nego. If he recovers, we'll bring him back, and no one needs to know what happened. We need to get the king away from everyone's curiosity. Let's not speak to anyone about this until we are certain of his status. Of most particular importance, let's withhold this information from your son. The next few days should make the situation more apparent. If this is the fulfillment of the dream, once we have the king placed safely and securely, we'll contact the twenty magistrates who witnessed the signing of the transfer of power."

"As you know, you'll have to be the one to let them know that the triumvirate will be ruling the nation for the foreseeable future. Though it will be difficult for you, I'm sure that I can count on you. All you need to say is that the issue regarding the king has come to pass and that we need to transfer the authority to the triumvirate. Tell them that you are conveying the information the king authorized you to give and that you can tell them nothing more than what he has authorized. Under no circumstances should you give any details about the king. Don't tell anyone. If someone seeks to express his sympathy, thank that person for his or her concern, but give no details, even if that individual acts like he or she knows. No one outside our circle should get any details about the king, particularly regarding his location. Prince Belshazzar should receive no information, no matter how much he pressures you. You must remain firm. The welfare of your husband and his ability to return to the throne depends on your strength and courage." By the time that Daniel had finished his instructions, the queen was still crying and shaking, but she had regained a measure of control and thanked us.

CHAPTER ELEVEN

The King in Hiding

THE KING WAS TAKEN TO MY HOME IN A SEMICONSCIOUS state. When he recovered full consciousness, he became wild and needed restraints. Try as we might, we could not control him without putting him in the chains that had been foreseen in the dream. As much as each of us wanted to remove the chains, we reluctantly concluded that they were necessary; the chains had to remain in place. He was taken to a shed I had prepared for him on the outskirts of our land.

Though he was uncontrollable with everyone else, he calmed down when Rachel placed her hand on his arm. She was initially nervous when she saw him, but her compassion overcame her fear. She reached out and touched the king's arm as she had that first time they had met. For the first time since the heavenly voice had sounded, the insane look upon his mien departed, at least partially. He calmed down and responded in a semi-reasonable manner. As the days passed, the same pattern continued. The king let Rachel touch him and even received food from her hands. He retained that civilized touch throughout his years of insanity, but in all other respects, he was like a wild animal. The clothing he had worn was soon in rags; within a few months, he was naked. He would allow no one to clothe him. His hair grew long and thick on his head and over his body. His nails grew out like claws, and they were potentially deadly to anyone but Rachel. Every day, she carried food out to him, and he received his food in a relatively tame manner. It was reminiscent of a vicious dog receiving food and affection from its master.

After three days of observing the king following the horrifying event, we concluded that what had befallen the king was the fulfillment of the dream. The queen notified the magistrates of the need to enact the emergency powers. The twenty men met with the queen, the prince, and Daniel to officially transfer the authority of the king to the ruling triumvirate, just as the document from the king had designated. Hananiah, Mishael, and I felt it was best if we were not present.

We took every precaution to prevent giving a hint as to the location of the king because we understood his degree of vulnerability. Many questions were asked. Daniel was impressed at how well the queen handled the situation. She acted far better than he had expected. She assured everyone present that the king was alive, but she adamantly refused to tell them any particulars about his status or whereabouts. When she was pressed from multiple directions, she declared, "The king has instructed me what I am to reveal. He is not able to resume his responsibilities, but I cannot tell you more. Please don't press me to go against his clear directions." Though many made the request, no one was allowed to see him. Prince Belshazzar was particularly adamant that he should be allowed to see his father. The crown prince petitioned again and again to know the location and have a chance to visit Nebuchadnezzar. The queen repeatedly assured him that the king was alive, but she remained firm in her refusal to tell him more. She would not under any circumstance allow him to see the king or ascertain his location. When the prince pressed her too vehemently, she went to the magistrates. They warned the prince not to exert undue influence over his mother. If he continued, he could lose his position in the triumvirate.

The hysteria of the queen that accompanied the king's initial distress continued to oppress her. Though she came periodically to see the king, his new persona was so completely unnerving to her that she could barely stand to be in his presence. Initially, she tried to speak with the king. Once she attempted to touch him, but the king became much more agitated in her presence. She was upset for days after the visit. In a short time, her visits became less frequent, and she gave up any attempts to interact with the king. She usually came during the night and quickly glanced at her husband so that she could in all honesty and confidence verify to the magistrates that the king was still alive. Every month, I gave her more detailed reports of the king's condition, which was derived mainly from Rachel's reports. Though I visited him regularly, the king was as agitated and dangerous with me as anyone else. Indeed, this was true of all other visitors except Rachel. She was the only one who could tell us anything more about the king than that he was alive.

Every month, the queen met with the magistrates. Though she was pressed to reveal the source of her information, she consistently replied, "Please don't press me. I'm giving you the information that the king has instructed me to give. I am telling you what he authorized me to say and nothing more. Under no circumstances will I divulge more than he has authorized." She assured them that the king was alive and receiving appropriate care.

The relationship between Belshazzar and Daniel became severely strained during their shared reign. Their positions in the triumvirate threw them into frequent and often intense conflict. The acting king was furious that the queen consistently refused to tell him the location of the king. Although he suspected that Daniel also knew the whereabouts of the king, Daniel consistently refused to confirm or deny his suspicions. The prince could never trick Daniel into revealing that he had any more knowledge about the king's condition than the prince. Belshazzar frequently queried whether the king was truly alive, even challenging the veracity of his mother. She assured the prince that the king was alive despite his indisposition. Though she had seemed so fragile when the king's sentence began, the queen proved surprisingly strong and resilient in fulfilling her role in the triumvirate.

Because he could not intimidate his mother into siding with him, Prince Belshazzar became enraged and bitter against our leader. He longed to vent his spleen against Daniel. The prince had several projects that he had envisioned implementing when he rose to the position of authority. With his father deposed, Belshazzar felt that he ought to have the authority to enact his dreams, but Daniel and the queen consistently thwarted his plans. Daniel allowed him some leeway in projects that did not conflict with Nebuchadnezzar's priorities, but in anything that was contrary to the king's plans or known preferences, our leader opposed the prince, and invariably, the queen sided with Daniel. Thus for the most part, all the grand designs and dreams of the prince were thwarted. Though initially Prince Belshazzar was thrilled to sit on the throne, wear the robes, and hold the scepter, he soon became dissatisfied because he could not exercise sovereignty over the realm, which those symbols represented.

Daniel had been the king's foreign representative whenever the king could not personally attend the situation and address the needs. Because he saw the prince's desire to impose his will on the realm without respecting his father's plans and desires, Daniel resigned his foreign position as soon as the triumvirate came into power. He was unwilling to leave Babylon because he feared the prince might be able to impose his will upon his mother if he vacated his position for any substantial length of time. The privilege of being the king's representative was offered to Prince Belshazzar. Initially, he was thrilled to have that responsibility, for in that foreign post, he possessed the authority of the king. However, he was suspicious as to why Daniel had offered the position, so he, too, resigned from the office. Mishael was appointed as the king's foreign representative. Because the policies of the triumvirate were conservative, fewer incidents needed to be attended to, but when the king's authority was challenged in a remote area of the realm, Mishael was sent, and he performed admirably.

Overall, the kingdom fared well during the seven years that the king was deposed. The army was sent forth to quell two rebellions that had erupted when rumors of the king's indisposition had leaked out. When those two rebellions were quickly and convincingly snuffed, the conquered subjects of the king realized that their rebellion would not be successful. There were no more attempts to throw off Chaldean reign. Daniel's conservative approach to governing the realm insured that no new lands were attacked. Twice, Belshazzar proposed sending troops into other lands to make further conquests, but each time, the queen sided with Daniel. After much whining and complaining by the prince, the measure was dropped.

Other than our ongoing concern regarding the king, everything in the administration seemed to go well, with the exception of Daniel's relationship with Belshazzar. The hotheaded prince never relented of his desire to bring the projects that he had envisioned to reality. He grew to despise Daniel for consistently thwarting his plans. Though he swore one day to have his revenge, he could not touch our leader as long as the triumvirate was in power. Had he attempted to usurp Daniel's power, he would have forfeited his position, as we made clear in the document that transferred the king's authority to the triumvirate.

CHAPTER TWELVE

The Return of the King

AFTER VISITING AND BRINGING FOOD TO THE KING EVERY day for seven years, Rachel was both shocked and overjoyed one morning to find Nebuchadnezzar sitting with a rational look upon his countenance. He had gathered some rags to cover his body and spoke intelligently. "When your husband and his friends made their plans for me, they expressed their confidence that you would be gentle and kind in your care for me. They never said how brave you were. That day I met you, you reached out in compassion to me, although I was the king. At the time, I appreciated the gesture. Though technically you were not supposed to touch the king, without question, I knew that you did so out of concern for my well-being. By that gesture, I knew then that you were the appropriate one to care for me. Though I have no idea how long I have been like this, my one pleasant memory through this horrible ordeal is you coming to see me every day. From the first, I knew you were gentle and kind. Now I know that you are also courageous. You're a perfect mate for your courageous and loyal husband. Please leave the food and tell Abed-Nego that the curse has ended. I need to be released from these chains and to get some proper clothes. Then I need to take some appropriate steps to prepare myself to return to the throne."

Needless to say, Rachel rushed to me with the news. After releasing him from his bonds and finding some suitable clothes for him to wear, we made the king comfortable in our home. Rachel gave him some decent food while I hurried to tell Daniel the news. The king embraced his trustworthy friend; they went into a prolonged and intense conference while still sequestered in our home. In meticulous detail, Daniel reported the status of the realm and the details about the major issues that had occurred in his empire. Despite his seven years of indisposition, there were few things outside the king's knowledge after spending two days in seclusion with his chief advisor. After listening to what Daniel said and noting what he did not say, the king asked, "How did my son comport himself in my absence?"

"The crown prince was a bit dissatisfied with me during your absence, Your Highness, but overall, he behaved well. He represented you in Susa once and in Damascus once, and he carried out his office well. However, he decided that leaving Babylon was not in his best interest. I'm sure that his primary motivation was his distrust of me. Following the prince's resignation, Meshach was appointed as your representative in foreign affairs. He's handled that office well when necessity called for him. Prince Belshazzar had several novel ideas about running the realm, but the queen supported me in blocking all those measures that would have resulted in significant alterations of the kingdom. In fact, I think you'll find your realm in relatively good order and not dramatically changed from the way you left it. The only battles we have engaged in were to put down two rebellions that occurred early on as the rumors circulated about you. Those uprisings were quickly overwhelmed. One occurred in Ecbatana and the other in Damascus, but those areas now seem as loyal to the king as ever," reported Daniel.

After feeling himself secure in the knowledge of the realm, the king sent for his barber, a loyal supporter, to help make him presentable again. With trimmed hair, beard, and nails and a fine set of clothes, the king sent for Arioch, the captain of his bodyguard. Arioch had remained intensely loyal to the king, always trusting in the king's return through all the uncertainty. He was overjoyed to find Nebuchadnezzar in full possession of his senses and up to date on all the pertinent facts of the kingdom.

The king's own bodyguard escorted him to the palace. The queen mirrored Arioch's reaction. Despite the reassuring portion of the dream, the queen had given up all hope of ever seeing the king as he had once been. She was overjoyed to see the king and amazed to behold him not just clothed and in his right mind but also fully comprehending the matters of state. Though Prince Belshazzar was notably less thrilled to see his father, he made as good a show of it as he could under the circumstances.

The following day the king met with the twenty magistrates (one of the original trustees had died, but his son had taken his place), thanked them for their loyalty, and made an official statement thanking the triumvirate who had governed so well in his absence. After that, the king mounted the throne and officially regained control of the realm. The final step was Belshazzar handing to his father the scepter and crown that had been his for seven years. Though it was easy to detect the reluctance in the prince's countenance to give up those royal emblems, Belshazzar handed them to Nebuchadnezzar with as much grace as he could muster and then embraced his father. Before all who were in attendance, the prince declared, "Welcome back, Abba. We all rejoice to see you recovered. I hope that your remaining years upon the throne will be plentiful."

Before the magistrates, his family, the four of us, and the nobles of the land, Nebuchadnezzar declared, "Though I have been humbled, in truth, I have been the beneficiary of these trying years. The lessons that I have learned from the hand of Adonai are profound and far more than compensated for the distress that I have experienced these seven years. Therefore, I bless the Most High God, to whom belongs all honor, blessing, and praise. Though I am the sovereign over my realm, Adonai is the only truly sovereign being. His dominion is everlasting; his kingdom endures from generation to generation. All the inhabitants of the earth are counted as nothing before the Lord. He does as he pleases within the host of heaven and on the earth. No one can ward off his hand or say to him, 'What have you done?' He humbles those who walk in pride. Though I've been humbled, I declare that Adonai has been good to me; he has treated me with a severe mercy. He brought me low in his justice, but he has restored me by his grace. All of his works are true, and all his ways are just. Though the lessons that I have learned have been painful, yet in truth, the Lord has been kind to me as well as merciful, for he has brought me to a knowledge of himself, the greatest treasure that any man can ever hope to attain. I praise and thank God for his wisdom and grace in his dealings with me."

Nebuchadnezzar reigned another twenty-three years. In the final decades of his reign, the Chaldean king gained far greater lands and power than he had obtained during his early years, stretching eastward as far as India, west to the shore of the Great Sea, and north even beyond the Black Sea. His realm was characterized by justice and fair dealings. Moreover, he remained true to his faith, worshiping the One True God for the remainder of his days.

Daniel was even more firmly established as the king's chief and most trusted advisor, but he was no longer the king's favorite companion. Rachel had usurped that position. Nebuchadnezzar was always appreciative of her care for him during his years of distress and treated her as though she was a favorite daughter. Hananiah, Mishael, and I were promoted to higher and more important positions within the king's court, although our authority and positions never rivaled that of our leader.

King Nebuchadnezzar's power continued unabated for the remainder of his life, but he was less inclined to exercise his power unless the situation forced his hand. The king treated all his subjects justly, but he was particularly good to the Jews. All the people in exile from Jerusalem were treated with favor and respect. Many of those who came to Babylon in a broken state and questioned whether they could ever recover had become the leading citizens in the Chaldean realm. All the blessings that God had promised for his people who settled in their new home in Babylon were reaped in abundance.*

Daniel contains many great events. Undoubtedly, many would consider the writing on the wall as a more appropriate climax for this second book, but I think the humiliation and restoration of King Nebuchadnezzar to be of greater significance. Some may challenge my conclusion that Nebuchadnezzar came to genuine faith, for he had made great professions after Daniel interpreted his first dream and after the trio survived the furnace. However, there was a qualitative difference in the attitude and words of Nebuchadnezzar after his humiliation. Though there can be no definitive proof, I remain confident that the Chaldean king truly came to faith. I expect one day to find him in heaven. Many of us have experienced God's severe mercy in our lives. Although our chastisement was perhaps not as severe as the king's, most of us can attest that Adonai's chastisement was both severe and kind, for the Lord teaches even as he chastises.

No mention is made of the steps that the quartet took to assure the king's restoration, but unless we are in complete denial, we must understand the difficulties that Nebuchadnezzar would have faced upon his return. The promise of the king's return was given in the dream, but it was appropriate for Daniel, Shadrach, Meshach, and Abed-nego to apply themselves to facilitate that return. Without question, Nebuchadnezzar was restored to the throne, but we are naive to think he faced no opposition. In many ways, the work of the quartet was like all the work of the kingdom of God. We know that God will bring his kingdom to fruition, but that confidence cannot lead us to passivity, for also know that he chooses to work through men. Like the quartet, we have the privilege of being God's coworkers in the vineyard, and he shares the bounty of the harvest with us.

Book Three
THE DEN

P ROLOGUE. FOUR YOUTHS (DANIEL, AZARIAH, HANANIAH, and Mishael) were taken against their will from Judea to Babylon, but despite numerous trials, they remained faithful to Adonai, the God of Israel. This Babylonian quartet was featured in Book 1, *The Furnace*, where their lives were threatened until Daniel told the substance and interpretation of King Nebuchadnezzar's dream. Later, Hananiah, Mishael, and Azariah, better known as Shadrach, Meshach, and Abed-nego, faced death for refusing to bow to the king's idol, but God spared their lives in the king's furnace.

In *The Restoration*, the members of Babylonian quartet were no longer young. Daniel was the second most important figure in Babylon (the king being the first). The other three also had prominent roles in government. All of them became critical players in King Nebuchadnezzar's court. When the king was troubled by another dream, Daniel again interpreted it, but the message was disheartening. Because of his arrogance, Nebuchadnezzar was humiliated and deposed from his throne. The quartet helped the king survive God's punishment for his arrogance and then took steps to ensure the restoration of the king following his seven-year debacle. After the great king was humbled, he came to true faith in the Lord. He returned to his throne; his reign was secure and he remained faithful for the rest of his life. *The Den*, also narrated by Azariah (Abed-Nego), takes up where *The Restoration* ends.

CHAPTER THIRTEEN

Shunted Aside

NEBUCHADNEZZAR DIED A CONTENTED OLD MAN, A KING who was much beloved by all his subjects. Chaldeans, those from foreign lands, and even the exiles, such as the Jews, who had been conquered by the Chaldeans and forced from their lands realized how fair, kind, and just the king had behaved toward them, particularly in his latter years. All his subjects seemed to realize how much worse their lot could have been if they had been under a different monarch. His death was mourned widely, sincerely, and officially for a month but much longer in most areas of the realm.

As hard as our great king's death was upon me, I think my wife, Rachel, took it more to heart. From the time of his restoration, the quartet were much more frequent guests in the palace. Nebuchadnezzar invited all of us to the palace when he had foreign dignitaries to entertain, but he also invited us regularly as his special guests. During those meals, the preponderance of his attention during those visits was on Rachel. In that dark hole that constituted the king's recollections of those horrible seven years of humiliation, Rachel had been the one bright spot for him. She was the only one whose touch he could tolerate. She had fed and cared for the king when all others were chased away. He rewarded her courage and diligent attention with an abiding love that continued throughout the remainder of his life. Indeed, as the king approached his death, he had Rachel attend to and nurse him. She was with him when he died, along with his wife and two eldest sons.

The crown prince, Belshazzar, eventually heard most of the details of Nebuchadnezzar's dream, its interpretation, and the role that my companions and I had played in that era of the king's life. Though Prince Belshazzar had acted as if he was glad to see his father restored, his act fooled few people of discernment. Indeed, upon hearing most of the details of the dream and plans put in place by our quarter from his mother a couple of years later, Belshazzar became so irate and belligerent with her and the four of us that Nebuchadnezzar sent him to Susa, ostensibly as the governor of that district but in reality as a warning to the arrogant prince. Rachel was present when the king told his eldest son, "Though I realize you have an enormous ego, you need to gain some self-control. It's clear to me that your anger at your mother and my four closest counselors stems from the role they played in thwarting your desire to usurp my throne. The steps that Belteshazzar and the others took were appropriate and demonstrated their loyalty to me, so ultimately, the anger you express to them is really directed against me. I am sending you to Susa as governor to give you a chance to gain control over your rage. If you don't learn to show substantially more control over your emotions, you might find that Susa is your permanent position. I have the authority and some inclination to anoint your younger brother to succeed me. I trust there is no need for me to speak more frankly."

When the prince returned, he was far more civil and outwardly submissive to the king and his mother, and he treated the four of us with restraint and some degree of respect. However, the anger that Prince Belshazzar harbored against the quartet was far from quelled during his exile in Susa. Instead, his rage simmered; his impotent anger at us grew into a permanent rift and deep resentment, which failed to dissipate to any significant degree by the time of the king's death. The prince demonstrated the necessary external show of acquiescence to the Chaldean monarch's rule, but his disdain and resentment toward our quartet were obvious and unabated. His hatred was most pronounced toward Daniel, who had thwarted his designs on the kingdom during the seven year hiatus of King Nebuchadnezzar's reign.

As Nebuchadnezzar felt that he was ready to go the way of all the world, he had a long discussion with his eldest son. The queen and Rachel were also there. From his deathbed, Nebuchadnezzar said, "Belshazzar, though I'm ready to go the way of all flesh, it's not too late for me to authorize a change in who will inherit my crown, so I advise you to listen carefully to what I have to say. You're poised to obtain the position for which you've lusted for decades. Though I realize that your desire to usurp the throne of your father is typical among princes, most crown princes are a bit more circumspect, a bit more politic in demonstrating their desire to replace their fathers. You were far too obvious about your resentment following my restoration, particularly toward those whose loyalty to me was most apparent. You may feel cheated because Adonai as blessed me with good health so my reign has lasted long. Without question, you feel particular resentment toward those who prevented you from taking absolute control of the realm during the seven years of my humiliation, but I recommend that you bury those feelings permanently."

"You'd better heed my suggestion to get control over your lust for revenge against those I value because I've made a plan to exert some control over you from the grave. I've given authority to the twenty magistrates to transfer the throne to your younger brother if you take steps to hurt those who arc loyal to me. The four Hebrew men who were brought here as exiles have been among my wisest and most loyal subjects. Without question, they have been my best counselors. Belteshazzar, Shadrach, Meshach, and Abed-Nego are men of true wisdom, deep faith, admirable character, and amazing courage. If you're wise, you'll keep them as your chief advisors, but I won't stipulate that much control. What I do insist is that you treat them well. None of their lands, houses, or possessions should be confiscated. They should continue to draw their full compensation from the realm. They've more than earned everything they'll ever receive."

"I reiterate that I've written these instructions out clearly for the twenty magistrates who have the power to replace you with my second son if you seek to harm those who have been so unstintingly faithful to me. Perhaps after you have consolidated your power, you may be strong enough to test your might against the twenty magistrates, but if you're wise, you won't attempt it. Must I speak more bluntly?" Prince

Belshazzar acknowledged that he understood the king's command and vowed to keep it to the letter, although no one thought he intended to keep us as his counselors.

After the funeral and official time of mourning were completed and the new king's coronation concluded, King Belshazzar summoned the four of us into his presence. He was brusque and to the point. After we made the appropriate show of obeisance, the king said, "Let's show each other sufficient respect to be honest during this brief but vital exchange, for I want the four of you to understand what your roles will be in my realm. Each of you held important posts in my father's court. He had great confidence and appreciation for you, but I'm not my father. He made me vow to treat you well. I plan to honor that vow, but I will do it in the manner that suits me. None of you will be my counselors. All of you will continue to receive the stipend you currently earn, but your positions within my realm will be largely emeritus. None of you will have the authority you formerly possessed. I trust you'll be able to reconcile yourselves to this new reality."

"I'm putting my friends in positions of power. They'll occupy your former positions within my administration. Each of you will have to report to men who used to be your subordinates. The reversal of roles may prove a bit challenging, but I'm sure each of you will be able to make the necessary adjustments. If you do nothing that suggests rebellion or disloyalty to me, I'll be content to leave you alone. You can take your ease from this day forward and know how much my father valued the contributions each of you has made to the realm. If I happen to need your services, I'll call upon you. Until then, accept my father's thanks for your service to his empire." The king looked each of us in the eyes, although he particularly looked at Daniel. Then he dismissed us from his presence. We were not surprised by his declaration and were careful not to say anything that might provoke the wrath of the arrogant fool who had ascended to his father's throne.

Instead of the diminution of our duties causing us undue consternation, we took the release from King Belshazzar as an opportunity to relax and enjoy our lives. The families of our quartet had been blessed; we became even more intertwined during this interlude of reduced pressure and expectations. My firstborn, Asher, had married

Mishael's second daughter, Tamar. Hananiah had adopted the two girls that my sister Elizabeth had had from her first marriage, and they had six more children. With fewer demands on our time, our quartet grew closer together during those years when King Belshazzar shunted us aside. We enjoyed the freedom from court intrigue and the intrinsic pressure that seemed to perpetually hound us as Nebuchadnezzar's counselors. Instead of precipitating feelings of resentment, the hiatus from intense activity felt like a reward for years of faithfulness. Though none of us felt that we had outlived our usefulness, we were content to do the work that was assigned to us and to let others seek to appease the arrogant king who was no longer young. Instead resenting reporting to men who formerly had been below us, we were glad to step aside, though we helped those who had leaped over us any time they requested assistance.

In many ways, Daniel had the hardest adjustment to make. First, he had no wife or children to make the transition more pleasant. He did use the time to become closer to each our families. Second, he had to transition from being the hardest-working man in the realm, the one with the greatest authority next to the king, to being shunted to virtual exile and idleness. King Belshazzar assigned Daniel a position, but it was so ill defined that no one, including Daniel, truly understood his responsibilities. In addition, all the lower administrators were intimidated by the position that Daniel had formerly held; they were afraid to assign him work, although he was ready to do any task that came his way. However, he found ways to make himself useful and remained content and confident that God's plans for his life were not over. The rest of us had administrative jobs, which were not as challenging as those we had once held, but we were at least somewhat productive and able to contribute to the welfare of the realm. Daniel had several visions during those years, which he shared with us. Though the visions were strange to my ears, we all recognized that God was sending important revelations about the heavenly beings and the future of our people to Daniel, so we encouraged him to record them.

My eldest son, Asher, who was named for my father, had worked in the same general areas with me much of the time since he was fifteen. Though I had endeavored to help him as much as possible during

Nebuchadnezzar's reign, the demands at work and concern about showing favoritism inhibited my instructions to some degree. Despite those limitations, Asher had advanced steadily through his own effort to a position of some prominence. Though I cannot truly claim to be glad to be shunted aside, a positive part of being demoted was that we all worked at a slower pace. In addition, having less authority meant I was in a better position to spend more time with Asher, instructing him in the more intricate details of our administrative responsibilities. No one worried about me at that point; everyone knew that I was not in a position to exert unwarranted favoritism. Though I did not deceive myself into thinking I could help him achieve a more desirable position in the current administration, my goal was for Asher to be fully prepared to serve in the administration of a different king, if that possibility arose, and I thought it likely.

Belshazzar was a petty man, unlikely to forgive the resentment that he had stoked for years against my colleagues and me, but he was no longer young and his dissipated lifestyle forecast a relatively brief life expectancy. Moreover, it was still my conviction that the best way for me to serve God was to work with appropriate diligence in my position, irrespective of the king over me or the reduced prestige that my position held.

CHAPTER FOURTEEN

The Writing on the Wall

THREE YEARS AFTER ASCENDING TO HIS FATHER'S THRONE and luxuriating in the position that he had coveted for decades, King Belshazzar hosted a great feast to celebrate his attainment. He invited nobles and counselors from his court and realm and some from foreign lands. He also included many who had been most prominent in the realm of Nebuchadnezzar, though he pointedly snubbed our quartet. If anyone was paying attention to such details, they could not have helped but notice that our names were absent from the guest list, but none of us were surprised or even displeased with the omission. We had no desire to be part of the celebration, and from all reports, the event had been stiflingly boring for the first two days despite the lively music and food sufficient to feed an army.

However by the third day, inebriation reigned; there seemed to be determination on the part of the king and his court to encourage reveling and at least give the appearance of felicity. By that evening, although the guests numbered more than a thousand, there were scarcely any sober men and few sober women in their ranks. The most obviously intoxicated of the lot was the king, who seemed determined to push the celebration into debauchery.

In the course of the celebration, an outstanding wine from Nebuchadnezzar's cellar struck King Belshazzar's fancy. He proposed,

"A toast to the gods of the vine who have created such an admirable drink. All the favored ones must partake of this noble vintage, which scarcely has a rival as far as its flavor and bouquet." As he glanced about for a suitable chalice to hoist before his admiring throngs, he declared, "Let's not insult this noble wine by drinking from chalices that are unequal to the honor. We'll delay our pleasure in partaking of this admirable drink while I charge my steward with the task of finding suitable gold and silver goblets to complement this outstanding vintage." The unfortunate steward made numerous trips from the palace to the courtyard, burdened by a variety of fine golden and silver goblets. Each was shown to the petulant king, but he rejected every one as inadequate. "Curse you, you fool," he shouted as he threw one of the chalices to the ground. "This outstanding wine deserves a proper vessel. To pour this wine into the cups you have brought would be an insult. You should lose your head for the suggestion. None of these chalices are sufficient to distinguish my father's choice wine in the manner it deserves."

Belshazzar began to grow sullen and dismayed. He was on the verge of despair when his mind suddenly recalled some treasures of old from his father's bounty. "Never fear, my fair guests. I have a plan to rescue this extraordinary wine from the insult of being served in an undeserving chalice. During his numerous conquests, my father plundered the Temple of Jerusalem. The gold and silver goblets he obtained from the Hebrews show exquisite craftsmanship, which is unequaled by those from any other nation. Steward, bring those goblets to us as fast as you can run, for my guests are becoming weary. When you return, we shall sound forth our toasts to the gods of the wine. When we've adequately honored this noble drink, we'll praise the gods of gold and silver that produce such noble chalices," he declared to great applause from his guests.

The goblets were brought, inspected, and admired by all those present who were still sober enough to participate. As the wine made its circuits, there was another surge of riotous drinking. Praise was shouted to the aforementioned, insentient gods, who could derive no pleasure from the accolades lavished upon them. However, to the One True God of heaven, the deity who knows every word in the minds of man before it is uttered, no acknowledgment was delivered by the king or his cohorts.

As the reveling approached its zenith, a large hand suddenly appeared out of the gloom. The disembodied hand started to inscribe a message for the monarch and all his arrogant guests into the wall that was opposite the king. The multitude of hands, which had been raised in tribute to the insentient gods, suddenly went limp and fell to the table. Many of the goblets spilled their noble contents on the table as the king and his guests were transfixed by the apparition. They stared as the enormous, detached hand inscribed their judgment for everyone to read. All were aghast. The king's face went ashen, and his eyes were bulging in horror as he fell back into his chair. To all appearances, King Belshazzar had already traversed the preliminary steps of being ushered into Sheol. Many of his guests wore a similar expression.

When he regained his voice, the king whispered to his closest servant, "Call for my counselors, Chaldeans, conjurers. Command them to come to me at once upon pain of death. They must read this inscription, for undoubtedly, it is a message from the gods for me." Then in the strongest whisper he could manage, Belshazzar announced, "If anyone can tell me the meaning of this writing, I'll adorn him with robes of purple that I've worn and a necklace of gold that has encircled my neck." The Chaldeans and wise men of the realm were ushered before the king in waves, but none could interpret the message. None of them could decipher the meaning of the enigmatic writing. As their failures mounted, the king became even more frantic and declared, "Anyone who is able to interpret this message shall be made ruler over a third of my kingdom." The added enticement was still insufficient to empower any of the Chaldeans to come to the aid of their king. As his escalating offers remained unfulfilled, the king's fear and despondency deepened.

The queen mother had made an appearance at the banquet earlier in the evening but had long since gone to bed, disdaining to participate in the debauchery that she was witnessing, although her son had authored the entire script. However, when word reached her regarding her son's distress, she returned to King Belshazzar. She was utterly disgusted to find the king crumpled up in his chair and acting as frightened as he had been as a child during thunderstorms. Her hauteur was visible to all as she looked upon the king's ghastly countenance and declared to her son, "Oh, king, live forever. Why have you allowed yourself to become so debased and humiliated before all your subjects? Your father was Nebuchadnezzar, the great king. Upon you rests the same authority that he used to wield. Surely, you've inherited enough of his heart and backbone to enable you to endure some adversity. Arouse yourself! How is it that you've allowed yourself to appear before all your guests as a child frightened by ghost stories?"

Though she hoped that her jibes would push the king to exert himself, the king sulked and looked even more disheartened as the jibes found their marks. Then the queen leaned over the king's chair and whispered, "Moreover, there's no reason for you to continue to be so distressed if you're willing to take a few appropriate steps. Though your favored counselors have failed you, there is another person in your realm who can come to your aid if you'll humble yourself and call upon him. When your father was truly perplexed, Belteshazzar was able to interpret his dreams and give him sound advice on more than one occasion, even after all his other counselors had failed. Humble yourself and send your messengers to appeal to Belteshazzar; he's able to interpret this writing on the wall."

Though the king could not help but remember Belteshazzar because they had been part of the ruling triumvirate for seven years, he held a grudge against his father's chief advisor. If he had had any other means of solving this dilemma, the king would have used it, but the enormous hand and its indecipherable message made him desperate. Belshazzar sent his chief messengers to appeal to the man whom he had so pointedly snubbed at the onset of his administration. When the messengers found Daniel, he was at my home.

Daniel asked me to accompany him to see the king. As we made our way to King Belshazzar, the servant told us all about the celebration, with particular emphasis on the events of the night. The servant had served directly under Daniel when Nebuchadnezzar was king and had loved working for our leader. He greatly favored his former boss to the men whom he currently served, so he relished giving us all the details of the king and his guests' distress.

When Daniel was ushered into the presence of the king, Belshazzar asked, "Are you Belteshazzar, one of the Jewish exiles brought from

Jerusalem by my father? My mother informs me that you have an extraordinary spirit. She claims that you can interpret dreams and discern all kinds of enigma. I have great need of those gifts at present. Indeed, I'd heard of your extraordinary powers even before the queen mentioned them to me." The king paused in his harangue to survey the effect his words were having on his old nemesis. Daniel looked at me and then over at the king but said nothing. His countenance was blank; it registered no emotions at all. The king's words obviously failed to impress him.

"At the present time, I have urgent need of your skills," the king continued. "I've asked all my conjurers and wise men to attempt to solve a riddle that imposed itself upon us. As you can see there, it's inscribed upon the wall opposite to us. All the wise men of my realm have failed me. Though I have made escalating offers, no one has been able to interpret the enigma. Therefore, I make the same offers to you that I made to my wise counselors." Again, the king looked desperately into Daniel's eyes, and again, he found no empathy in the countenance of the man whom he had so demonstrably snubbed. Finally, the king admitted, "Belteshazzar, I truly need your help. You were a friend as well as a counselor to my father. For his sake, will you help me?" In the last part of his proclamation, the look of fear and desperation had returned to the king's face, and his voice was tremulous.

As Daniel observed the desperation in the countenance of the king, he softened toward the son of his former close friend. "You have no need to bribe me to obtain my service. As I served your father, I'll serve you. Your father was the great king—the greatest in all the land. However, the one who brought about King Nebuchadnezzar's ascent to fame and power was Adonai, the God of Abraham, Isaac, and Jacob. Because of the grandeur and authority the Lord granted your father, Nebuchadnezzar ruled the entire world. When the king made a decree, it was carried forth without delay. If he declared a man would die, that man would not see another sunrise or even taste another meal. If he extended mercy to the man, he lived unmolested and unchallenged. If the king chose to make a man great, that man was favored for life. If he chose to humiliate anyone, that man was cast down forever and without hope of recovery."

"However, because of his greatness among men, King Nebuchadnezzar elevated himself in his own mind. He deceived himself into thinking that his power and authority arose from his own greatness. For that reason, God humbled him in a dramatic manner. Though I repeat this story to you, you are fully aware of what happened. He became like an animal. He was chained, fed on grass, and exposed to the elements for seven years until he acknowledged that Adonai was the Most High God."

Daniel continued, "Your father learned his lesson, and his kingdom was restored to him. As his son and heir to the throne, Nebuchadnezzar's lesson should have served to instruct you. Although you've observed all that happened to your father, you haven't benefited from the instruction, which so dramatically played out before you. To entertain your friends and exalt yourself in their eyes, you made toasts to the gods of wine, gold, and silver—insentient objects with no ears to hear or eyes to see. Then you showed your disdain for Adonai, the One True God, by drinking from goblets stolen from his temple as you praised the inanimate gods. King Nebuchadnezzar learned obeisance and trust in the Lord, but you've shown your disdain for the only true God, the one being in all creation with ultimate power. As a consequence, while you were in the act of elevating yourself over the Most High God, he sent the great hand to inscribe your judgment on that wall. Therefore, hear the judgment that Adonai has made known to you and your guests. The hand wrote, '*MENE MENE TEKEL UPHARSIN.*' *Mene* means your days are numbered, and they have come to an end. It is repeated to let you know both the certainty and imminence of the sentence. *Tekel* means you have been weighed in the balance and found wanting. *Upharsin* means your kingdom will be divided between the Medes and the Persians." Daniel finished his pronouncement and looked about with disdain upon all the guests.

When Daniel finished speaking, a pall fell over the king. In his gloom, King Belshazzar brooded in silence, as did his guests. After prolonged deliberation, the king rose from his chair and declared before all his guests in a subdued tone but sufficient that all could hear, "Belteshazzar, what you have declared is true. I own it all. The One True God has justly and rightly condemned me. I, the son of King Nebuchadnezzar, refused to obtain wisdom from the events of my father's life. Instead of gaining insight into the truth and humbling myself before the One True God, as my father did, I was peeved that I was denied the opportunity to exercise my authority during the seven years of my father's humiliation. Although I knew that the sentence Adonai imposed upon my father was because of his pride, I failed to benefit or gain wisdom from his humiliation. I've been a fool of the first order. May God have mercy upon my soul, even as he extended grace to my father."

After delivering his soliloquy, the king sat down, and he was lost in his despondency for several minutes. Then he roused himself and ordered his servants to bring out the robe and golden necklace that he had vowed to give. Belshazzar put them on Daniel and declared, "From this moment forward, Belteshazzar will be regarded as ruler over one third of my kingdom. All my subjects will show to him the same honor and obeisance that they show me."

CHAPTER FIFTEEN

The Medes and Persians

THE INSCRIPTION ON THE WALL FORETOLD KING Belshazzar's doom. The prophecy for the son of Nebuchadnezzar made it clear that a swift and decisive end to his reign was imminent. Five hours after Daniel gave the king the interpretation of the writing, the Medes and Persians overran the kingdom of the Chaldeans. King Belshazzar died in the attack. Had he truly repented and grasped the grace that Adonai held before him? I hoped so.

That fateful night, there was an overthrow of the world. Shortly after Nebuchadnezzar had mounted the throne in Babylon, the Chaldeans had become the leading power in the world, replacing the Assyrians and Egyptians in their battle of Carchemish. The Chaldeans' reign continued throughout the life of Nebuchadnezzar, but the night of the handwriting on the wall, the Medes and Persians became the reigning dynasty, soundly defeating their rivals, culminating with the overthrow of Babylon, although clearly the decisive battles of the conquest had taken place earlier. Undoubtedly, the forces of the Medes and Persians had been routing the outposts of the Chaldeans even as Belshazzar had entertained his friends and toasted the insentient gods rather than attending to issues of state. While the king was promoting reveling, his father's realm was snatched from his hands. If the son of Nebuchadnezzar had warnings about what was happening on the battlefield or the danger that lay just ahead, he had ignored the reports or treated them with disdain, as though his hauteur would be a sufficient weapon to defeat any enemies. Any knowledge Belshazzar had of the pending invasion died with him that night. By the next morning, the reign of the Chaldeans was over.

The Jewish exiles in Babylon who had survived the siege of Jerusalem were paralyzed with fear as the Medes and Persians overran the country. The assault reopened emotional wounds that everyone hoped had healed. We quickly came to realize that the healing had been superficial and insufficient. The scars were rapidly opened, revealing the raw sores upon their souls. I saw the trauma renewed upon the countenances of the members of mine and Rachel's families—even in Rachel. Their minds flashed back to Jerusalem; memories they had attempted to wipe from their minds reappeared as they anticipated a return of the horrors that they had experienced during the siege. Fortunately, those horrors never materialized in Babylon. Though the new conquerors killed King Belshazzar and many of those who were prominent in his court, they had no desire to inflict widespread destruction of chaos. Babylon was captured by the Medes and Persians without having to resort to siege. The battle had hardly been engaged when the war ended. Instead of inflicting harsh punishment and widespread destruction upon the capital of the Chaldean realm, the Medes and Persians sought to incorporate Babylon as one of the leading centers of their kingdom, although the capital of the Medes and Persians' empire was Susa.

Our conquerors were committed to making the transition back to a stable government and productive society with as little chaos as possible. Provincial governors came in within weeks of the Chaldean dynasty's fall with the goal of mollifying the populace and finding suitable workers for the new administration. Interviews were conducted by their staff. Those selected as suitable candidates were interviewed by the governors themselves. Announcements were made to the general population, assuring them of the new administration's humane intent. Multiple posted announcements read, "Citizens of Babylon, if you are peaceful and productive, you have nothing to fear from the Medes and Persians. Our goals are for a rapid transition back to peace and productivity." Though the panic and distress induced by the conquest was intense, we were all back on our feet within weeks. Our families were able to adjust to a new ruler and way of life with only moderate upheaval of our sense of security and well-being.

King Darius, a Mede, became the new ruler of the realm. Though the Medes and Persians conquered the empire set up by Nebuchadnezzar, they actually held the Chaldean king in great respect. In particular, King Darius admired the way that Nebuchadnezzar had treated the intellectuals from the kingdoms that he had conquered. Following the example of the Chaldean monarch, Darius intended to bring qualified candidates from other cultures into the realm of the Medes and Persians. So as King Darius began his rule over the former Babylonian empire, he set up a tribunal to look for suitable candidates for his court. All those who had been in the court of Belshazzar or Nebuchadnezzar were interviewed. Those who were bright and willing to serve the new administration were given the opportunity to earn a place in his court. Daniel, Hananiah, Mishael, and I were treated affably. After appropriate interviews, we were offered positions in the Medes' administration. Each of us gladly accepted. What else could we do? There was no Jerusalem to receive us back.

The governor himself interviewed those selected from among the former high-ranking officials. He was particularly interested in those who held prominent positions within the court of Nebuchadnezzar. When he spoke to me, he asked, "Why is it that after you held such a high position of trust in the administration of Nebuchadnezzar, you were virtually dismissed from the court of Belshazzar? Why did the son of Nebuchadnezzar have so little confidence in you and your three colleagues?"

Though I sought to evade the answer, the governor had a lot of information at hand and kept confronting me. Eventually, I had to tell our story, starting with the interpretation of the two dreams. That led to our role in facilitating the return of Nebuchadnezzar to his throne after his humiliation and the resentment of Belshazzar for our interference with his plans to usurp his father's throne. The governor was impressed with the trust that the king had extended to us and the wisdom that we had demonstrated in bringing about Nebuchadnezzar's restoration. When he spoke with Daniel, he received a consistent story, although

Daniel revealed to him more about my role in the plans for protecting Nebuchadnezzar and help in his restoration. Hananiah and Mishael were also interviewed, and the governor got a good overview of the role that each of us had played in Nebuchadnezzar's administration. At the end of that process, the four of us were retained in relatively high positions in the Medes' administration. Hananiah and Mishael were selected to stay in Babylon; they were placed near the top of the administrative pyramid, holding positions of similar rank to what they had held in Nebuchadnezzar's administration. They performed the same tasks for the Medes that they had previously done for the Chaldeans. They reported directly to the provincial governor who forwarded their work to Susa.

Both of my friends were pleased to stay in Babylon. They felt settled in their work and communities. They preferred to not have to uproot themselves again. My mother, Ruth, elected to stay with Hananiah and Elizabeth rather than face immigrating again. She had stayed with my family from the time her her exile from Jerusalem, but she felt the transition to a new city at her age was too difficult to contemplate. I thought she chose wisely. Moreover, Elizabeth felt that Mama had been in my house long enough. Her family wanted their turn of hosting the matriarch of our clan. It was difficult for Rachel, the children, and I to say goodbye to Mama, for we realized that there was little likelihood that we would ever see her again. Our chagrin was offset by the excitement of a move to Susa and opportunity to continue and deepen our relationship with Daniel.

CHAPTER SIXTEEN

Gaining Ground in Susa

ANIEL AND I WERE SELECTED FOR THE KING'S
administration in Susa, and I was able to get my son Asher a
position working under my supervision. Uprooting from our
home was difficult, particularly with the prospect of leaving Mama
behind. I had lived in Babylon three times as long as I had lived in
Judea, but I was pleased to be selected for the honor of serving in King
Darius's court. From the first, I admired the king. I saw many parallels
between this new Median king and the strengths that I had noticed in
King Nebuchadnezzar. But the main attraction was continuing to be
with our leader. Daniel had become a vital member of our family. Of
our quartet, he was the only one who had never married. Though he was
close to all of us and deeply loved the Hananiah and Mishael's families,
he spent more time at our home. I always sensed that Daniel felt more
comfortable with our family. He felt welcome to drop in unannounced.
My children called him uncle. We had a room for him anytime he
decided to stay over.

Since I refuse to live in denial, I was neither surprised at being
chosen to go to Susa nor at Daniel being placed in a higher position in
the Median government. Though I am clever and possess considerable
talents and abilities in the administrative realm, I had known from our
first days together that Daniel's mind and talents far exceeded mine.

Though I spent my life around men famed for their intelligence, I never met anyone close to being the equal of Daniel. He was too good for the Medians to pass over. The king quickly discovered his abilities. King Darius set up a pyramid hierarchy of the 120 satraps who were brought into his court at the conclusion of the interviews. About one-third of the satraps chosen for the pyramid were Medes, one-third were Persian, and one-third were from the exiles of the various lands conquered by either the Chaldeans or the Medes and Persians.

After the initial interviews by the governors, Daniel was the highest ranking of all the exiles, but his initial appointment was in the middle of the pyramid. Knowing Daniel as I did, I was sure that he would have been content in the middle of the hierarchy, but Daniel was far too talented to be squandered in such a low-ranking position, as King Darius quickly discovered. The monarch conducted his own interviews as people from various sectors of the kingdom made their way to Susa. At the end of Darius's selection, both Daniel and I were promoted. Following that intervention, I became one of higher-ranking men from among the exiles. My promotions put me somewhere in the middle of the pyramid. Daniel was promoted to one of the top ten positions in King Darius's government. Those ten men met regularly with the king. They had the authority to either deal with issues appropriately or direct the issues to the king. Over the next year, both Daniel and I rapidly advanced in our language capacities so that we became relatively fluent in Median, the official language of the realm. As Daniel's language skills increased, his intelligence, insight, and administrative abilities became more obvious.

By the time King Darius had been the ruler of land for two years, he had trimmed his inner circle to three men. Daniel was one of the three highest-ranking satraps. Ironically, the promotions were of little concern to Daniel, whose primary concerns never included riches, recognition, or fame. He probably would have been content to stay in Babylon. He was clearly content in each of the positions in Susa, but his honesty, wisdom, industry, and clarity of expressing ideas caused the king to continually promote him in the interest of the realm, and for his own benefit. As he more appropriately utilized Daniel's talents, King Darius's own responsibilities were simplified. Much of the tedium could be entrusted to Daniel, who would see to it that the vast majority of issues received appropriate treatment before reaching the king. He could be trusted not to ignore truly vital concerns, and he consistently weeded out less vital issues without troubling the monarch.

By the time we had been in Susa three years, King Darius had decided that Daniel would be his primary minister. The king hated dealing with inane matters. His expectation of the move was to make it so he would no longer be afflicted with ridiculous ideas. The plan for the evolving administration was that the lower satraps would report to one of five highly ranked officials in a new inner circle. Those five would deal with all routine concerns. The more important questions would then be brought to Daniel, whose responsibility was to deal with those issues as he saw fit. He would handle the majority himself and only bring to the king those issues and petitions truly vital enough to warrant Darius's input. Therefore, three years into the reign of the Medes and Persians, the gradual shifts in governmental structure that were introduced by King Darius brought Daniel to the verge of assuming the same position he had been in under King Nebuchadnezzar: second in authority for the entire realm.

Such promotions do not go unnoticed; Daniel's promotion was not greeted with favor by the ambitious, which included virtually all of those in the king's administration. Though I was far lower in the pyramid than Daniel, I frequently felt the sting of jealousy from the middle-ranking satraps when I was promoted over them. By that stage, I was positioned over about half the Medes and Persians in Darius's court. Just as it had been in Babylon, there was enormous jealousy and contention regarding my position; I sensed constant whispering behind my back. Since that was my experience in the middle of the pyramid, I could only imagine the amount of jealousy Daniel had endured in his promotion to the top ten and then the top three. I dreaded to consider the reception that he would receive when the king announced his appointment as the prime minister.

In one of Daniel's regular visits to our home, I asked, "What's it like at the top of the pyramid? Though I constantly feel the resentment from the men over whom I have been placed, my authority is relatively insignificant compared to yours. You must feel like you being constantly scrutinized by those who are jealous of your success."

Daniel laughed and said, "You're completely right. As you can imagine, those who have been in the inner circle were men of great ability and even greater ambition. They were not happy when I was chosen to be in the circle of ten. They resented having a Jew among the leaders of their country. When King Darius made me one of the three in his inner circle, I felt a commensurate increase in their ire. Therefore, I shudder to think what their reaction will be when he announces that he has chosen me as his primary minister, the one to whom the inner circle of five reports. From you, I get nothing but sincere congratulations and joy, but your family may be my only well-wishers in Susa besides the king. I have mixed feelings about the new post because I understand the king's motivation. Without question, there are ways I can serve the king better in the capacity that he envisions, but I dread dealing with the inevitable jealousy that will arise."

"I'm sorry to hear about their jealousy, although I'm not surprised. I can only imagine the pressure you feel," I replied. "The promotions I've received pale considerably when compared to yours, but with each promotion there is sufficient rancor that I sometimes envy the relative stability that Hananiah and Mishael have experienced by remaining in Babylon. Tell me about the king. Why is he taking this step?"

After a couple of minutes of contemplation, Daniel responded, "King Darius reminds me of Nebuchadnezzar in many ways. He's enlightened. In many ways, he's kind and generous, but his ego is just as massive as Nebuchadnezzar's. The main reason he wants me as prime minister is so that he doesn't have to waste so much time hearing the various inane ideas or complaints from those in the inner circle whose selectivity he feels is suspect. The king trusts my judgment. He's convinced I'll bring to his attention every vital idea and concern. Probably more importantly, I'll spare him the inane and mundane. Nebuchadnezzar also hated to be tortured with ridiculous ideas and foolish requests. I functioned in much the same capacity in his realm. By the time I reached that position in Babylon, we had been through the ordeal of the first dream. All of Nebuchadnezzar's counselors owed their lives to us, as much as they desired to forget it. Though they did not like my ascendancy, they tolerated me. Moreover, Nebuchadnezzar made it clear that any challenges to my authority would be treated as rebellion against him."

"The Medes and Persians feel no attachment and have no obligations to me. In the position that the king foresees for me, the vast majority of proposals from lower officials will receive an appropriate dismissal before reaching the king's ears, which will make his life simpler. However, I know that my new position will make me less popular with the other satraps, especially those closest to the top. Comparing King Darius to Nebuchadnezzar, I sometimes worry about Darius's ego. As you undoubtedly recall, Nebuchadnezzar's elevated view of himself brought the Chaldean monarch down for those seven years. Though I certainly hope nothing like that occurs in this kingdom, I see the similarities between the monarchs. Without question, Darius relishes praise, as is probably true of all kings."

"A humble king—could there be such an animal? The little I've seen of Darius makes me like him, but I'm sure he has no lowly view of his worth or abilities. I presume you have no choice about the promotion?" I asked.

"None. When the king discussed the idea with me, I tried to dissuade him. I suggested to him that he could utilize my talents in the manner that he foresaw without making the position official; I encouraged him to officially keep matters status quo. As we discussed the issue, I stressed to the king how poorly my promotion would be received, particularly by my two colleagues who will unquestionably view the change in their positions as a demotion. However, the king is really sold on the idea. He feels that unless the position is official, the other two will seek to bypass me so that he will still have too many inane ideas from my colleagues in the inner circle. He looks forward to escaping from the mundane proposals that those advisors bring to him. Moreover, he is convinced that the animosity my appointment generates will dissipate quickly, but the benefits will persist. Though I hope he's right, I don't share his optimism, for I know the men who will feel demoted. I have already felt their jealousy as rumors have started to circulate," said Daniel, who was uncharacteristically despondent as he contemplated his future role.

Again, I was struck by the uniqueness of my friend. I think any other person in the world—myself included—would see the promotion as a well-deserved affirmation of the work that he had done in both Babylon and Susa. However, Daniel was different from anyone I had ever met. I really believe that in his striving for excellence, he had little ambition except to honor God. In his mind, the new honors that would come upon him would not balance out the animosity and antagonism that he would face from his former colleagues.

Two days later, I sat in a dark corner of my favorite inn drinking tea. The day had been hectic. I needed some relaxation and separation from my work. Though I brought along some work to consider, I was actually thinking about the conversation that I had had with Daniel regarding his pending promotion. In particular, I was pondering what a unique man Daniel had to be. His tremendous abilities had greatly impressed two kings of opposing realms, yet he seemed to be void of ambition. He would prefer to avoid his upcoming promotion. Was there another man like him in all the world? All of a sudden, I overheard a conversation between two men who were sitting relatively close by. Though they were attempting to whisper, their voices carried surprisingly well. If the men saw me at all, which was unlikely, they did not realize how easily I overheard their conversation.

Having no desire to eavesdrop, I was about to move away when I heard one of them mention my friend in a contemptuous manner. He said to his colleague, "Heaven be praised. I'm convinced we've finally trapped that Hebrew upstart Daniel. We tricked King Darius into signing an order according to the law of the Medes and Persians that should permanently remove that thorn from our sides." Concern for Daniel prompted me to stay and listen more closely.

His companion replied, "Excuse my skepticism, but how are you going to trap Daniel? Have you ever looked at his ledgers? He's extremely careful, and by all I can discern, he's completely honest. He works tirelessly, and he is utterly loyal to the king. If you're thinking about getting someone to tempt him with a bribe, save yourself the bother. There's no way he'd ever consider taking a bribe or even let you trap him into appearing to take one, for he's also unusually discerning. If you're considering other means, I think it's even less likely he'd ever be entangled in adultery, irrespective of the woman you recruit to entice him. Though I'd love to see that arrogant Jew brought down, I don't see how you can do it."

"Every man has his weaknesses and vulnerabilities. Though everything you said about Daniel is true, even he has his susceptibilities," said the first speaker. "He is utterly devoted to the Hebrew God, as he demonstrates every day."

The second speaker replied, "His devotion to the God of Israel is fairly common knowledge. Indeed, I suspect his devotion to that Hebrew deity is at least part of the reason why the schemes I've mentioned would fail. How do you plan to use his devotion to your advantage?"

The first speaker chuckled maliciously to himself and said, "Yesterday, I went with six other men to the king. We spouted our praise regarding Darius' wisdom, being, and majesty. We were so effusive in our flattery that I was afraid he would see through our scheme, but the king simply soaked up the compliments as his due. As you know, the Medes believe that the king descends from the gods; I think Darius really believes it. His arrogance was foundational to our plans. After a prolonged recitation of his great deeds, we assumed a position of extreme obeisance and told him that he was the only deity in the kingdom worthy of worship. At the conclusion of our praise and flattery, we got him to sign an injunction against anyone making petitions to any god or deity other than him for the next thirty days, according to the law of the Medes and Persians, which cannot be revoked. Anyone making such a petition will be thrown into the king's den of lions."

"And everyone who knows Daniel knows that he prays to his God three times a day," replied the second man, with excitement entering his voice for the first time. "Let me congratulate you. That was a brilliant stroke. Indeed, your plan may give us the means of silencing that troublemaker for good. But let's not start rejoicing too quickly. Don't you think that when Daniel hears about injunction, he'll only stop making his petitions to his God for that month?"

"Not if I know Daniel, and I do," the first speaker said. "I've worked closely with him for the last three years. He nauseates me with his virtue, but he's as stable as a mountain. He never varies from his routines. Unless I have totally misjudged him, he'll continue to make his petitions, even if he hears of the law. If he does, we'll trap him. I think it's a virtual certainty."

As I listened to their diabolical plans, I felt queasy. They were right about Daniel. He was so predictable and faithful that I agreed with the first speaker's assessment. I would go to Daniel and reason with him, but I was not optimistic. How likely was I going to be in getting him to alter his practice? Even if he knew about the trap, Daniel would probably continue to pray, but I felt it incumbent upon me to tell him of the plot and try to persuade him to take steps to thwart their plans. Though I was also dedicated in my prayers to Adonai, continuing the pattern that the four of us had established when we had arrived from Jerusalem, I was not the one that they sought to entrap. Perhaps they might go after me later if their ploy with Daniel succeeded, but it was clear that my friend was their primary target. Daniel was the reason that they had tricked the king into signing the law. He would be the one that they would discover disobeying that law unless I succeeded in getting him to alter his routine.

I left from the inn as unobtrusively as I could, but I could not help stealing a glance at the conspirators. The men were Shethar and Admatha. As I glanced their way, they saw me. Both Shethar and Admatha had been members of the original ten in the inner court. At that time, they had been equal in authority to Daniel. I have no reason to think that they ever really liked Daniel, although the one time that the ten of the inner circle had entertained the lower satraps, there had been an appearance of goodwill among them. Along with Daniel, Shethar had been among the trio that had been selected as the king's inner court, whereas Admatha had been overlooked. According to the rumors that were abounding at work, both of them were to be among the five who would report to Daniel when they attempted to reach the ear of the king, but clearly neither of them was content with that arrangement.

There was little reason to think that they would know me. The lordly ones of the inner court tended to make a point of failing to remember the lower satraps unless they perceived that recalling the name of an inferior might be to their advantage. My concern, however, was that I was the only other Hebrew among the 120 satraps. If they recognized that I was an Israelite, they might suspect that I was a friend of the one they sought to entrap. My glance was but momentary as I exited the inn, trying not to give the impression that I had overheard their conversation or that I was more than passingly interested in them. I made a feint toward the building where I normally worked. When I could no longer be seen by those who were in the inn, I headed straight for Daniel's abode. I only looked back once as I turned toward Daniel's home. I did not see either of the men with that glance.

As I approached Daniel's home, I slowed my pace and glanced stealthily around. I saw no one. If Shethar and Admatha suspected me of overhearing their plot, they were taking no steps to intercept me from warning my friend. My first conjecture was probably correct. They did not recognize me as one of their fellow satraps. When I got to the house, I found Daniel alone. He had just completed his prayers to Adonai, and he was eating a simple meal when I came upon him.

When I burst in upon him, I was clearly excited and probably a bit incoherent in my report. "Daniel, I have just come from an inn. As I sipped on tea, I happened to overhear Shethar and Admatha discussing a plot they are hatching against you. They have tricked the king into signing a law according to the Medes and Persians, which says that anyone who is caught praying to another deity for the next thirty days will be thrown into the king's den of lions. They came up with this plot to trap you because they know your routine." I was still somewhat breathless in my excitement, but my friend did not seem as bothered by my report as I had expected him to be.

After pondering my announcement for a moment, Daniel surprised me by asking, "Azariah, you've just told me that people who hate Adonai and oppose me are hatching a plot to kill me. Though I appreciate the information and your concern, I'm wondering what you would have me do."

Stunned by his question, I answered sharply, "You need to be wise. You need to out maneuver them and avoid their trap. The wisest step would be for you to alter your routine for a month. Adonai will certainly understand; I think that he would even approve of your wisdom." Daniel's mien was blank, so I proceeded, "Look, these men have set a plot to destroy you by using Darius's ego and your devotion to Adonai. You know as well as I do that the king would never have signed the law or done anything that would allow them to hurt you if he had understood their proposal and design. King Darius was blinded by their flattery. If you won't think about yourself, think about the king and the distress this trap will cause him. All that I'm recommending is that you change your routine for one month. Pray earlier or later. For a month, you don't need to be so demonstrative and open. You've led an amazing and faithful life. There's no reason why you should allow these jealous men to succeed in their vicious plot. The alteration in your schedule wouldn't be such a big change. It would only be for a month."

"Something like bowing my knee to an idol just one time," he said, smiling at me. I was struck mute by his reference. "So you don't think I have the faith that you, Hananiah, and Mishael demonstrated years ago?" he asked innocently.

As I recovered, I replied, "That was a different time and situation."

"How so?"

"When we heard about the idol, we tried to avoid the summons to the plain of Dura. After we were forced to go, we didn't want the king to find out about our refusal to bow before his idol," I replied. "If we could have avoided the summons by the king, we would have."

Daniel smiled. "Of course, you would've. You were seeking to be faithful—not defiant—but you refused to bow to King Nebuchadnezzar's idol, even when he offered you a second chance. Though I'm not surprised you never mentioned your adventure in the fiery furnace to me, did you really think I would fail to hear about that great demonstration of faith and courage by my three closest friends? You trusted Adonai, and he intervened for you. Even when you were quite young, the three of you were ready to die for your faith. Indeed, you would have died had the Lord not intervened miraculously on your behalf. Now I'm an old man. I was sixty-five when Darius came to the throne. You don't think I can let three twenty-year-old boys show me up in the area of faithfulness, do you?"

My friend had me. He and I both knew it. After pondering the predicament, I admitted, "It appears that I can say nothing to persuade you. Though I don't agree that the situations are the same, I understand your point. If you're determined, I'll respect your decision and cease my protest. However, I'm going to the king first thing tomorrow and see if I can intervene for you. And my family and I will pray for you."

"Both will be appreciated," he said; we hugged and I departed.

CHAPTER SEVENTEEN

The Lion's Den

FOLLOWING THAT CONVERSATION, I TRUDGED HOME dejectedly. There was no chance that I could get in to see the king that evening despite what I perceived to be the urgency of the situation. Although there was a possibility that I might be able to intervene and warn King Darius of the plot by going early the next morning, I knew that the odds were against me. My political influence was minimal. When I told Rachel what I had overheard, she sent word for our children and grandchildren who lived nearby to come and pray for Daniel. Rachel and I had had eight children, although two had died before reaching the age of five. Three of our children lived in Susa, having moved with us from Babylon. Asher, our eldest child, had six grown children. We had twelve grandchildren living in Susa, four of whom had reached maturity.

Our children and their spouses plus the four oldest grandchildren came over that evening. We prayed to God to thwart the evil plot of Shethar and Admatha. As we poured forth our prayers for our leader, the prayers of my children and grandchildren moved me. I could tell by their heartfelt petitions that they felt as attached to Daniel as I did. His death would be as painful for them as it would be for me.

The next morning, I rose earlier than usual and arrived at the king's palace before daybreak. As far as I could discern, I was the first arrival that day. Though I had been to the king's residence a few times, I was by no means a frequent visitor. By my reckoning, if I arrived before everyone, I would have a better chance of being ushered in to see the king. After I explained who I was and my urgent need to see King Darius on business that directly impacted the king, his servant escorted me into an outer chamber. Several minutes later, a lower servant brought me tea and flatbread. Like Daniel, I had never been overly concerned about my place in the hierarchy of the government, but that day, I felt my lack of prestige and authority most acutely. After I had been exiled to that outer chamber for more than an hour, I beheld Shethar and Admatha with six other men being greeted with profuse kindness and respect by the same servant who had shunted me to the periphery. From the obvious tone and the few words that I overheard the servant utter, I gathered that the servant was only too pleased to usher the octet directly into the presence of King Darius while I nibbled on stale flatbread and drank lukewarm tea. A few moments later as I languished in that outer chamber, Daniel was hustled into the presence of the king flanked by six soldiers. The octet was still with the monarch. After a heated exchange of words, my leader and friend was marched out again between the same soldiers. The performance made the reality clear; I was accosted by the recognition of my own futility. The plot of Daniel's enemies had clearly succeeded while a sipped on lukewarm tea.

Though I understood fully that my attempted intervention had failed, I continued my vigil of waiting for my conference with the king. Two hours later, I was finally ushered into the king's presence. Though King Darius was not nearly as enormous as Nebuchadnezzar, he was still a large, powerfully built man. But that day, his appearance struck me differently. The king was slumped in his chair. His countenance was sullen and wan. When I was finally ushered into his presence, the first words out of the king's mouth were, "What time did you come to the palace today?"

"Your Highness, I arrived before daybreak. I believe I was the first visitor to the palace."

"You came to warn me about the plot concerning Daniel, did you not?"

"Yes, Your Highness, I did. Yesterday as I was having tea, I overheard the details of the plot against Daniel. Shethar and Admatha were discussing how they had tricked you into signing the law that forbids the petitioning of any deity other than yourself. I wanted to see if there was any way that I could get you to retract the order before they succeeded in trapping my friend."

The king looked down and shook his head. "How could I have failed to see through the ruse of those flatterers? What was it about my ego that made me delay seeing you although the servant informed me that you had information that impacted me personally? When that small group of conspirators came in this morning, even a blind man should've been able to penetrate their ploy. Shethar said, 'Oh, king, did you not sign a law prohibiting your subjects from petitioning any god other than yourself for thirty days?' Like an imbecile, I traipsed right into their trap by replying, 'Yes, according to the law of the Medes and Persians, which cannot be set aside.' Then they informed me that Daniel had been caught that very morning praying to the God of Israel. Having played into their hands as readily as they could have wished, I was bound by my own stupidity. I had no choice but to order Daniel's arrest. At sunset this evening, he's to be thrown into the den of lions in accordance with the law of the Medes and Persians, and there's nothing I can do to spare him."

I informed the king, "After I overheard Shethar and Admatha discussing their plans to entrap Daniel, I went to him in the evening seeking to persuade him to set aside his prayers to Adonai for a month. Though he knew about the plot, he was unwilling to alter his routine." Then I told the king about the adventure Hananiah, Mishael, and I had experienced when we refused to bow to Nebuchadnezzar's idol. "The God of Abraham, Isaac, and Jacob spared my colleagues and me. He can also spare Daniel's life. We'll continue to pray that he does." The king was somewhat mollified, but only just. He then surprised me by asking me to accompany him as he sought legal advice regarding the situation.

Although we saw four different leading experts on the law of the Medes and Persians that day, not one of them gave any hope of sparing Daniel. The fourth advisor told us plainly, "If someone has violated an ordinance signed as the law of the Medes and Persians, no one— not even the king—can interrupt the proceedings of the law. The king has no authority to free that person. However, the king—and only the king—can rescind the law if he feels that it is unjust, signed in anger, or enacted without proper consideration. If the king rescinds the law, no one else can fall victim to it, but anyone already in violation must suffer the consequences spelled out in the ordinance."

When King Darius understood the provision, he declared, "I hereby rescind the law concerning the petitioning of any god other than me for thirty days."

The expert of the law replied, "Your Highness, I have heard your official declaration. We can now consider that law null and void. Though I wish I could offer more help to you at this time, I cannot. Though the law can no longer be used to trap anyone else, I regret that your declaration cannot save your servant Daniel, as much as I wish it could." At the king's request, I stayed with him for the remainder of the day.

That evening, we went to see my friend. Ironically, Daniel looked better than either one of us. I felt wan, but the king's countenance and posture were pathetic and pitiable. He said to Daniel, "My foolishness and cursed ego have brought you into this predicament. Though I have been tricked by flattery into executing this sentence, perhaps your God, whom you continually serve, will be able to protect you from the lions. I've discussed the matter with every legal advisor and pursued every avenue possible. It is clear that I have no power to free you from this sentence, which I have unwittingly imposed upon you." After the king and I had hugged Daniel, Darius reluctantly gave the prescribed order. The door to the pit was opened; Daniel was tossed into the den of lions. Darius thanked me for accompanying him and returned to his palace. I returned to my home to report the failure of my mission.

When I told her of my dismal adventure, Rachel said to me, "When you and your friends faced the fiery furnace, you hoped God would intervene to somehow keep you out of the furnace, but he didn't. Instead, he let you be tossed into the flames, but he met you there and kept you safe. Last night, we prayed that God would thwart the designs of Daniel's enemies. Accordingly, you went to the king, hoping you could persuade him to change the law before Daniel was trapped, but in that venture, we failed. However, I still believe Adonai may intervene for Daniel. My prayer is not only that the God of Abraham, Isaac, and Jacob will spare his life; I'm also praying that Adonai will meet Daniel in the lion's den the same way that he met you in the flames. Indeed, when I can get you to speak of that day in the furnace, you say that it was the greatest day of your life because of the way the Lord met you there. That'll be our family's prayer tonight." Our family again came together to petition the God of Israel to spare Daniel's life. We fasted that evening and night and then went to bed. We rested fairly well despite our anxiety over the danger our friend was facing.

The next morning, the king rose early from a restless night. His servant arrived at my home before sunrise with a message from the king, requesting me to join him immediately at the lion's den. When we met at the door to the pit that contained the lions, the first rays of the sun were shining in the east. The sun had barely crested the horizon when the king gave the order for the door to be opened. King Darius called down, "Daniel, servant of the Most High God, has your Lord been able to protect you from the lions?"

I can scarcely relate the wonder and blessedness I felt when we heard, "Oh, king, may your reign be long and prosperous. Adonai found me to be righteous, and I was innocent of any plot against you. My God intervened and kept me safe. The lions have not touched me. I haven't been injured at all."

Our prayers had been answered as completely and dramatically as the time when the three of us had been thrown into the furnace. When I heard Daniel's voice, I shouted, "Hallelujah, praise the Lord," and the king ejaculated the same words of praise immediately after me.

With the assurance that Daniel's life had been spared, King Darius turned his attention to settling the rest of the matter. Having already rescinded the law, the king summoned the flatterers to the palace to face him. He asked me to be present as he confronted the men whose conspiracy had forced the king to sentence his chief advisor to death. "You worthless dogs. Azariah overheard your plot, which was as much a treacherous attempt to overthrow our realm as it was a cowardly plot to harm Daniel. Though he sought to intervene for his friend, Azariah was too late to warn me about your scheme. Your plans were too well thought out and executed for his intervention to succeed. Though you sought to make a mockery of me and used your flattery to get me to condemn an innocent and righteous man to death, the One True God intervened. Daniel slept in the lions' den and emerged unharmed because of his trust in the God of Israel. My suggestion to each of you is that you now call upon your gods to see if they'll protect you in the same way that Adonai protected Daniel."

Then the king called in his guards and had the men taken to jail to wait until sunset. Toward evening, the king again invited me to accompany him. I watched as the king gave the order. Each of the conspirators was cast into the pit, but none of them even reached the bottom. The hungry and enraged lions tore the men apart, leaving nothing but shreds of their clothing.

The following day, Daniel came to our home and thanked us for our prayers. My children and grandchildren were gathered there to greet their "uncle." There was great rejoicing and many tears. Daniel hugged and thanked each of them personally for their petitions on his behalf. Then to all of us, he declared, "Thank you, my dear family. I'm convinced that Adonai spared my life because of your prayers."

Later that evening, Rachel and I were able to be alone with Daniel for a time. I asked, "What was it like in the lion's den?"

Daniel was a quiet but intense man. He looked at us and said, "It was an amazing experience. Instead of being consumed by fear, my time of being with the lions was the best night of my life. In truth, I had no desire to leave the den when King Darius called out to me. Unlike what I've heard of your experience, there was no visible person in the den with me, but I felt the presence of God more palpably than ever before—even more than when he gave me the interpretation of the dreams or the visions. I'm sure it was similar to your experience in the furnace. Of course, those men hated me. Their whole purpose for entrapping the king and me was to end my life because of their jealousy, but in fact, God turned their plot upside down. My night in the lions' den ended up being the greatest blessing that I've ever known. It was a foretaste of heaven. I experienced a closeness to Adonai that I had never known before."

CHAPTER EIGHTEEN

Conclusion

KING DARIUS'S LIFE HAD BEEN TRANSFORMED BY THE entire experience. Throughout the tumultuous process, he experienced a gamut of emotions. Because of his own ego, he experienced the shame of falling into a trap that his disloyal subjects had set. He knew the misery of ordering the execution of a man whom he greatly loved and respected and the anxiety that flooded his mind and resulted in a sleepless night as he awaited the confirmation of his friend's death. On the following morning, he felt the elation of hearing Daniel's response from the den and the satisfaction of justly sentencing the conspirators to the death that they had sought for Daniel.

However, the strongest and most overwhelming emotion that King Darius experienced was the awe of realizing that there truly was a God in heaven who was all wise and powerful. He had discovered a deity with sufficient power to protect his servants, even when they were cast into a den filled with ravenous lions. As had been true with King Nebuchadnezzar, King Darius's experience had humbled him. Fortunately, he was awakened to the danger of flatterers. He was made vividly aware of the vulnerability that was caused by his own ego.

After the king dealt with the traitors who had attempted to trap him into killing his most loyal and able servant, he assembled all the hierarchy of his government and the nobles of the land to announce what had occurred and utter a proclamation before them. Among all the satraps who were present that day, there was a great show of loyalty to the king and support for Daniel as his prime minister, even though the sincerity of a significant number of those present was questionable. I believed that many in the government were afraid that they too might find a bed with the lions, for the conspiracy was not limited to those who were executed. However, the king felt enough blood had been shed. He did not launch an exhaustive search.

Though the primary purpose of the ceremony was to announce the restructuring of a new government, the king used the occasion to make another announcement. "May peace abound to each of you. Many of you are aware of the horrible conspiracy that threatened our government. By seeking to destroy Daniel, the conspirators sought to hurt and possibly destroy me, for Daniel is my most able and trusted counselor. However, the leaders of that conspiracy have received their just due. They met the end they envisioned for Daniel. Though Daniel was innocent of any plot against me or anyone else, the conspirators entrapped me into throwing him into the lions' den, but he was protected by Adonai. The God of Daniel intervened and protected his servant."

"Therefore, I make the following proclamation to all my subjects. All men throughout my realm are to fear and reverence Adonai, the God of Daniel and the true and living God who endures forever. His kingdom will never be destroyed or superseded. His dominion will continue to advance forever, irrespective of the opposition. The Lord performs wonders in heaven and on earth. He protects his servants who trust in him. He delivered Daniel from the lions' den and restored him to his place of honor. All the earth belongs to the God of Israel. All my subjects will worship and honor him from this day forward." King Darius then announced the appointment of Daniel as prime minister and the five satraps in the next highest rung. This appeared to be unanimously approved by all who were present. The king surprised me by appointing me to be among the five satraps in the next highest rung of government.

EPILOGUE

The Babylonian quartet continues to amaze us with their courage and faith. In reality, the scriptures are silent about Azariah (Abed-Nego), Hananiah (Shadrach), or Mishael (Meshach) after they survived Nebuchadnezzar's furnace, but it is incomprehensible that they would fail to remain faithful to Adonai. There is every reason to expect that they would continue to serve God and the Chaldean realm. We know about Daniel. He lived throughout the entire circuit. The quartet were among the first people that were taken to Babylon, probably around the time King Jehoiakim provoked the Chaldean king by withholding the tribute that was due. Though Daniel was not mentioned as being with the other three when they were thrown into the furnace, it is inconceivable to me that Daniel would have bowed to Nebuchadnezzar's idol. Instead, I had Nebuchadnezzar send him away during that time, which I consider to be a feasible explanation.

Without doubt, Daniel was one of the most powerful and influential men in the realms of the Chaldeans as well as the Medes and Persians, which was an amazing accomplishment for a foreigner from a conquered land. After the night with the lions, Daniel continued to serve in the administration of the Medes and Persians. We are told that Daniel lived until the reign of King Cyrus, the great Persian king, during whose reign, the Jews returned to Israel, and the restoration of Jerusalem was begun. It takes little imagination to envision Daniel playing a central role in persuading King Cyrus to take the lead in the restoration of Israel to the Promised Land. Although he was probably taken against his will, Daniel (and perhaps his companions) survived the seventy years of Israel's exile, and they were used by Adonai to bring about the conclusion that God had intended. Daniel's life was full of courage, wisdom, and faithfulness; he continues to be an encouragement for all of us who live in an era when the worth of those virtues is minimized. We need to be continually inspired by the Babylonian Quartet.

Printed in the United States
by Baker & Taylor Publisher Services